The Orange Sky

I0682570

Anant Parasher

First published in 2017 by

Becomeshakespeare.com
Wordit Content Design & Editing Services Pvt Ltd
Unit - 26, Building A-1, Nr Wadala RTO, Wadala
(East),
Mumbai 400037, India
T:+91 8080226699

Copyright © 2017 by
All rights reserved. Any unauthorized reprint or use of
this material is prohibited. No part of this book may be
reproduced or transmitted in any form or by any
means, electronic or mechanical, including
photocopying, recording, or by any information
storage and retrieval system without express written
permission from the author/publisher.
Please do not participate in or encourage piracy of
copyrighted materials in violation of the author's
rights. Purchase only authorized editions.

©
ISBN: 978-93-86487-35-3

DEDICATION

To my dearest Bauji, my Late grandfather and my greatest inspiration and source of strength, thank you for all your kind blessings and we hope you keep a kind watch over us, *always*.

To the Almighty, whom I owe everything.

ACKNOWLEDGMENTS

THIS BOOK WOULD NOT HAVE BEEN POSSIBLE WITHOUT THE SUPPORT OF my parents, Dr. Divyanshu Parasher and Dr. Rajni Parasher, without whom this would have simply been a dream. To my Dearest Grandmother, who has always loved me more than herself, I would like to pay my humble gratitude. I would also like to thank with all my heart, my soon to be life partner Jeplin, who gave me the enormous amount of confidence needed to pursue this endeavor once again.

A special thanks and a vast amount of appreciation towards Dushyant Uncle and Ravi Uncle, whose reviews and healthy contributions always guided me towards writing a more vibrant story. Last, but in no way the least, A special wave of gratitude towards my Dear friends Praful Rai, Rupak Chowdhary, Gaurav Singh and Raman Ghai for giving me encouragement and support through all the good and bad times we had together.

TO THE CREATIVE TEAM AT BECOME SHAKESPEARE AND WORDIT CONTENT DESIGN SERVICES, I WOULD LIKE TO EXPRESS MY MOST HEARTFELT GRATITUDE TOWARDS EVERYONE INVOLVED IN THE FRUITION OF THIS LITERARY WORK

CONTENTS

(1)

*June 25*th *2010*

Present Day.

'*Don't say it......I already know*'..............these are the last words I hear before the chirping crickets in the tranquil night become silent and the beautiful face I had held in my hands, melts into an intangible mess on the front porch. It's the same dream I've been having since it happened about two months ago, always ending with me waking up in a cold sweat and my heart wanting to burst out of my chest like a man kept against his will and forced to do a job he is too tired of doing anymore. It was a warm early summer morning in Delhi as I checked the clock that told me it was too early to get up anyway. Instead of going back to sleep, I lit a cigarette and took a deep drag. I coughed furiously for a while, each breath as unforgiving as the last one and my chest wanting to rip itself in half. After managing to finish the last puff, I sat on the bed for about five minutes just staring at the mangled pieces of cement that was supposed to be a wall, just hoping that maybe this was all a bad dream and I would actually wake up soon. After tasting bile at the back of my throat a few minutes later, I got up from the sweat-drenched bed.

Looking into the mirror that day, I had trouble recognizing the face that I had seen every day for so long as I can remember. It was a man standing in front of me who was clearly not in his senses. Weary and tired blood shot eyes and a beard just a few inches shy of making me the new entry into the Taliban. I had not eaten proper solid food for the past few weeks and had lost a lot of weight. Before going to work I thought of eating something and glanced inside the fridge, which offered me nothing but a half-eaten pizza from a few days back, the sight of which churned my stomach. 'I can't do this anymore' I muttered to the empty kitchen as I kicked the fridge shut.

Working in a hospital was, well to say the least, a little depressing. I mean you really chose the wrong day to be a doctor if you ever needed a little humor for the soul someday. I was working as a second year postgraduate in Internal Medicine in BHK Hospital, Shahdara. It was quite decent considering it was a government setup and like every other setup had its share of crap infrastructure. Moreover, I had not become a doctor because of some dire need to help the needy or contribute to society in any way. I became a doctor because of the same reason almost everybody else does- Money (was pretty naïve, did not know any better at that time) and probably because i wasn't good at anything else. To say that I had disintegrated my social life in the past five years or so would have been an understatement. Society thinks doctors have it all, a huge bank balance, golf on the weekends and the works; the reality is sadly different. The only respite I ever got once in a blue moon, was when a patient was somewhat grateful for treating him, otherwise it just feels like being in a monotonous panorama of futility.

The Medicine department was on the seventh floor of the hospital and as it is with elevators, they hardly ever work. Just seems gravity is just too good for them sometimes. After just three floors and many curse words, I was ridiculously out of breath. Now, I wasn't out of shape or anything but as any chronic smoker would vouch for, stairs really are your worst enemy. Somehow, huffing and puffing I reached the seventh floor with my head just about to explode. I reached the nurses' station, popped an aspirin and gulped down half a liter of water. Rounds had already started and after seeing the look on the face of my senior consultant, I knew this just wasn't my day....it hadn't been my day for a while now.

"Dr. Arjun, so glad you could be here today", he said looking unflinchingly at his watch and then at me. "We certainly are a privileged lot, aren't we!" making no attempt to hide his sarcasm, the smug bastard.

This is the thing with doctors. No matter how much you achieve, it all comes down to shit in one bad day. After a few awkward glances and listening to a few snickers, I joined in the crowd of interns, some undergraduates and a few of my senior residents. Amidst the crowd of patients, the first year postgraduate was nervously handling the files of each patient and trying to jot down investigations and other stuff; desperately trying not to dig a hole and hide his head in it. I made my way through the crowd as we moved on to the newly admitted patients.

"Kishori Lal, 68 year old male admitted with severe abdominal pain and bloody vomiting..." squeaked the first year PG.

"Oh boy Ajju, this must be your lucky day." said a voice behind me.

Without turning my head, I knew it was Vibhor, mostly because nobody else calls me 'Ajju', not their fault actually; it's a bloody stupid nickname. Vibhor was just one of those people who for some reason, have been in your life for so long, that even if you don't even like them, it'd be really weird not to call them your friend. It wasn't that he was repulsive or anything, but let's just say I had a little trouble adjusting to his quirky personality .We had been together during our all years as undergrads and somehow with his luck or mine, now post graduates in the same hospital in Internal Medicine. *It's a small world after all.*

"Why? Did you decide to leave medicine and start gratifying older women?" I just couldn't help myself.

"No man, guess I was too big for them....but you'll do just fine." The smartass had an answer for everything.

"One of your favorite cases, this Kishori Lal.

A chronic *bewda*....you just love those don't you!" he said giggling like a little girl.

Great, just fucking great. Just what I needed right now. I hated alcoholics and I mean I really hated them. Don't get me wrong, it's not like I was really pious or virtuous about it and sure, there may have been a few occasions when I had puked my guts out after a 'social gathering'. However, something about an alcoholic really pissed me off. Be it their wife beating, constant delusions of grandeur or just their utter vainness to the world. As I began to size my new patient from head to toe, I saw nothing different from the rest of them, except for a painfully silent expression. He had his face turned away throughout the examination and did not respond to any questions thrown at him by my overzealous residents. Somehow, in a strange way, he reminded me of myself at that point in my life. After rounds got over, I went to work up the new admissions on my own and gave the first year postgraduate hamster his share of the wheel on which he'd be running all day.

"Hey look what I found on the internet dude!" my eardrums vibrated with Vibhor's irritating voice. "Two monkeys smoking grass man!" his excitement was that of a teenage girl.

"Get lost Vibhor, and turn off this shit." I grumbled as I flicked his phone across the table.

"Hey, don't be an asshole okay. By the way, what has been going on with you for the past couple of weeks? Are you okay? You're always late nowadays and what's up with this Osama look, huh?" he said.

"It's nothing, just leave me alone and go suck up to your senior resident or something."

"Good idea man, I could use some brownie points with Dr.Thakur, last night I forgot to take a complete work up of a patient and he ended up vomiting all over Thakur's new leather shoes, you should have seen his face dude." he giggled.

After he was gone, his question was still with me. "Are you okay?" I thought to myself if this was how it felt being okay; life wasn't worth living at all. *So no, you're not okay,* my brain reassured me. I filled the new patient's investigation forms and put them in his file. As soon as I got up to pass over the file to the nurse in charge, I suddenly felt a jolt of dizziness limping through my brain. I caught hold of the corner of the table and steadied myself, at the same time noticing the gaze of the group of junior nurses who had been interrupted from their daily dose of gossip. The nurse in charge picked up the patient file I had dropped on the floor while on my vertigo trip.

'Doctor Arjun, no breakfast today as well? I see you're making a habit of it.' the nurse said in a calm voice.

'Don't worry *sister ji* ....I'm fine, just lost a little balance there.' I tried to defend myself.

'Nothing doing, here I brought some sandwiches from home this morning, have a little something to eat.' She said as she offered me a blue Tiffin.

'Aap nahi hote to main kya karta sister ji' (What would I have done without you) I said as I took a cucumber sandwich from the Tiffin.

'Okay okay....enough with the buttering up now. Go lay down for ten minutes and I'll fix up the chart for this patient.' She said almost ordering me to go.

'You are the best *sister ji*' I said with my mouth full of moist bread and cucumbers.

Sister Rina had always been a good soul. A widow of about fifty, she had been working in the hospital for about twenty five years or so. Being the most experienced of the nurses' lot, she commanded respect from almost everybody- be it the nurses or the consultants. Being a kind woman at heart too, she had always given the most support to the first year postgraduates. I definitely was a challenge to her, with my constant doubts in diagnoses and changing patient's drug regimens all the time. But I had made it through somehow and I owed a lot to her. Every once in a while, when she used to be on night duty, we used to have little chats about useless topics just for the sake of it. She lived with her two sons in a small apartment near the hospital and talked for hours about how she wanted to make them both doctors. A perfect woman for the job, I guess.

I took a sip of water to dissolve the ashy taste of my morning cigarette and the sandwich combining into an acid reflux and pushing it down momentarily, I headed to the duty room. I opened the creaky door and saw a bunch of juniors, mostly second year MBBS students creating havoc inside. They saw me enter and thinking I probably just wanted to use the loo, went back to their frenzy. A student, fresh off the gym douche bag brigade, gave me a sly look while enjoying the company of his chirping female batch mates. I knew I had to lie down for a while or else I'd feel like pulped sugarcane. But no one had said I couldn't have my fun with the little piggies.

"Which semester?" I demanded sternly.

For the first time that I had stood there, everybody sat quiet and looked at me. I sat on the table beside the bed and read their faces. One of the bespectacled bookworms said in a tiny voice-

'Third semester sir....medicine posting from 9 to....1.'

"Do you know the meaning of the word posting?" I asked the young caterpillars some of whom were searching the ground for something now.

"Should I talk in Hindi if you dumb heads don't understand English?" I was probably screaming but didn't notice.

"We were just waiting for somebody to take our class." The pea brain athlete said looking to act tough for his crowd.

You dug your own grave son; it's my duty to put you in it.

"Oh I'm terribly sorry to hear that you had suffered such inconvenience. Maybe I'll just line up the patients for you and explain what's wrong with each of them. How about that, It'll be fun, won't it?"

Most of them had understood where this was going and had buried their faces in their books. But I had to make a lasting blow.

"*Beta*, this is Medicine. Nobody can teach you and nobody will teach you. Read your theory and see the patients for yourself instead of gossiping like teenage girls." I realized I had been going on for a while.

'I have read the theory part.' the stud said triumphantly.

"Okay, then you'll have no problem in telling me the various liver function tests and their normal values, will you?"

I got my dues as I watched the blood draining from his face and him trying to match the stares of his fellow mates.

'Sir....uh....I....its....' he started to mutter.

"Exactly that's what it is, and don't forget it *bachhe.*' I said with authority.

"Now pick up your books and get out of here. Evaluate the liver failure patient in bed eight and write a decent history. I'll see it in twenty minutes."

The room was empty in five seconds and I finally found a pillow for my aching head. I pushed the bags aside to make some space, sending some books to the ground in the process. I didn't bother to hear them hit the floor or to even pick the ones I heard dropping. I was tired, too tired to think of anything. To think of the million little insignificant, trivial and inconsequential things people worry about each and every other day of their pathetic lives. Too much garbage in the world, I had always thought to myself. **Welcome to life…..don't forget to take your share of the shit. Make it last now…and please suffer in small installments**. That must've been the tagline when they first manufactured life in a little container. But, I guess that's what any other bloke must've thought when in this situation. I kept one hand on my tightly shut eyes and let the other hang from the side of the ramshackle bed hoping in vain to lose consciousness at some point.

Sleep didn't come and I laid there feeling like death would be such a sweet relief right there and then. It didn't have to be dramatic, just quick and efficient enough to get the job done. I rolled around in the bed for a little while and finally gave up. I opened the bathroom door and put my half-empty packet of Marlboros on the sink. After bolting the door from inside and opening the unsteady window (which creaked like a dying rat) somehow, I took out a fag and dragged in deep. My throat burned as the smoke made its way through it, poking and prodding every inch on its way as the tobacco fumes slowly made their journey out the window. I grunted as I flicked ash into the toilet bowl and pressed the flush lever, which as I found out, had some other plans.

I finished the cigarette and spent the next two minutes chewing a mint gum and letting the exhaust work its magic. I splashed some cold water on my face and rubbed my eyes, which had turned to cherry red. After two hard slaps on both cheeks to gain full orientation, I walked back to the ward.

I had to work up the new patients before rounds the next day. As I was already on thin ice with the consultants nowadays, so i decided not to delay the matter. The new admissions were placed in a separate room called the Annexe, which was more of an extension going perpendicular and right to the main ward. The new patients were there for a few days only before their work up was completed and diagnosis made. I made my way to the Annexe and walked up to Bed no.10. On seeing me approach, the person who had come along with the patient stood up and greeted me with folded hands.

"Kishori Lal?" I confirmed just for the sake of it and sat on the small stool near the bed.

'Yes doctor *sahib*, this is him. My name is Bhola, I'm his neighbor.' He said while still standing with hands folded and gazing at me expectantly.

"Sit down and wake him up, I need to ask him some things." I said without looking up from my sheets.

'Doctor *sahib*, he's does not talk much to anybody now. Would you mind if I were to answer your questions?' he was almost pleading now.

I was already having a bad day and did not want to entertain this kind of behavior from a patient.

I was about to throw a fit when I looked up at the man who had brought the alcoholic. Roughly forty or so, he barely had a covered torso with a thin sheet of ancient ruins of what used to be a *kurta* and whatever was remaining, was drenched in a hard day's sweat.

From one of the places the cloth was shredded, I could see ribs projecting out in a ghastly way. I looked down, and he had nothing to cover his feet and the bruised soles glanced at me with disdain. A man of such limited means, probably not even having enough to feed his own kids, and here for somebody else, just begging for a decent worth of my time. *I just had to add guilt to my day's orchestra of emotional burden.*

"*Theek hai,* that's fine." I said almost apologetically.

I took the history from him as possibly accurate as I could; all the while trying not to think about the ice picks poking into my brain each time I opened my mouth to say something. The patient had the history of every alcoholic I had ever come across in the time I had spent in this hospital. It was the same old story of clinging to the bottle and increasing the amount of useless garbage on this planet. I finished up and saw the nursing orderly walking up to the patient with the food tray. I signaled him to show me the food chart and gave my approval. As I was about to get up and leave, I heard a splashing sound too much familiar to the ears of every child who has ever done some tomfoolery in his childhood and at the same time felt something warm and moist on my groin. The *yellow dal* from the food tray had made its way onto my trousers, which were completely drenched till the knee. In addition, the white curd had trickled down to my shoes that now looked like a hazy zebra crossing on a busy street.

"Damn it....what the hell!" I blew a fuse.

I looked at the nursing orderly with what would have appeared to him as two fiery red flames in a boiling cauldron. He just stood there and looked at me with whatever decency he could muster up. As I looked around, I saw the other patients watching this midafternoon soap opera.

'Sir...I...I....was giving the patient.....' he stammered.

"Giving the patient? Did you see the patient sitting on my lap there?" I demanded a futile explanation.

'Sir....I was giving the tray and he refused to take it. I'm sorry that I dropped it on you, doctor *sahib.*' he said not meeting my stare.

"Well if he doesn't want the food, then don't give him any. It's not as if it matters to me if he eats or not. Bloody free food and service to these people and they take us for shit." I wasn't screaming but my fried brain and parched throat made me feel as if I was hearing somebody somewhere scratching a ceramic plate repeatedly with a fork.

I stood up with my edible trousers and started to walk away. After I had a glass of cold water and calmed down a little, I told the nursing orderly to clean up the mess and bring a fresh tray of food for the patient. I didn't mind his bewildered expression when I told him to do so. After a while, I went back to the annexe entrance and called out the attendant.

'Doctor *sahib, maaf kar dijiye...master ji aajkal nahin jaante wo kya kar rahe hain*' (Please forgive us, nowadays he does not know what he is doing) he pleaded.

"I shouldn't have shouted Bhola; it's me who has to apologize." I said as I held his trembling hands.

"I'll send another doctor to do the examination in a while, help him however he needs it." I said, as he looked bemused at my confession of guilt.

I kept my hand on his shoulder and reassured him that I would be back later on to check on the patient. He thanked me and went back with what I noticed for the first time was a limp in his right leg. *'The patient is your god Arjun, treat him like you would treat god if you ever met him'* the words of my late mentor echoed in my mind repeatedly.

After finishing up case studies for my thesis, I was in no shape to do anything else for the day. I called Vibhor and asked him to take the new patient rounds. It was 5.30pm and I knew I had to face the evening rush hour traffic to reach Karol Bagh, which was certainly worse than ever every time you were in one. I reached home around 7pm and parked the car near Bittoo's tea stall. The stall, originally named Ramchand's Tea stall, had been there when my father and I had had shifted here about twenty years ago and was still running well in the small neighborhood it served. The owner of the small enterprise, Ramchand babu had changed the name when his wife belonging to some small village in Uttar Pradesh had borne him a son, whom he named Bittoo. Ramchand was like any other man in the mid sixties – poor, but making an honest living. He had also been on good terms with my father, and whenever I had a craving for some chocolate cream biscuits, we would come by his shop. I used to see them together as not just acquaintances, but more as two friends sharing a joke over a candid evening's cup of tea. Recently his condition had gone south and he didn't come to the shop often, which left his son, Bittoo in charge. Following in the footsteps of his father, he too had the same keen sense of business and close relationships. He used to work all week from six in the morning to eleven at night and on weekends, had been attending some basic Verbal English course; paying for it by the money he had saved up from his teashop.

'*Bhaiya ji*, how are you...I have not been seeing you for some days now.' He greeted me with the usual optimism and a beginner's accent in his voice.

"I'm good Bittoo, was just a little busy. I see the English lessons are paying off pretty well." I said as I surprisingly got offered a firm handshake.

"Hey, that's quite good. I think you'll surely impress some *videshi* madam, eh." I said with a sly smile.

'*Aisa nahi hai bhaiya ji, bas thoda thoda aata hai* (It's not like that , I don't know much but just a little)' he said blushing a bit.

"Well, keep working at it and you'll be great."

25

'Thank you *bhaiya ji,* please sit down and I'll make you a cup of hot tea with *elaichi,* just the way you like it.'

"Not today Bittoo, have to see *papa*. Some other time, maybe."

'*Theek hai bhaiya ji.*' He said feeling a little disappointed.

As I walked a few paces to the end of the curb where Bittoo's tea stall stood, I heard a loud *Bhaiya ji!* and on turning back I saw Bittoo hurl something at me. I caught the gold plastic wrapped five star and looked at him.

'I hope it is still your favorite!' he shouted.

"It is and always will be Bittoo." I said as I winked and forced a smile. I realized how you could not put labels on some relationships.

My father had retired from his job at the bank and was now living on a fixed pension. I tried many times to help out financially as I was making good finally but he never accepted a penny from me. 'I don't have anything to spend on, what will I do with the money' Was what he used to say to make my efforts futile. A few weeks after I had gotten admission in postgraduate medicine, I had taken up a flat on rent, near the hospital with Vibhor. I knew I had needed it badly because of my hectic schedule and because the traffic between the hospital and my place in Karol Bagh, was certainly a bitch. The thought of leaving dad alone ate at me, so I had hired a domestic help to cook and clean up around the house.

I walked up to the house and noticed something that froze my steps before the front porch. It was a fragrance, a sweet scent that was all too familiar to me but had not caressed my nostrils in what felt like a long while. Then, it hit me like a freight train running from reality to a world where absurdness had taken over. *White lavenders*…..but how was it even possible? There were no lavenders of any kind nearby or for that matter, even anywhere near where I had lived. The best floral shop for white lavenders was some place in the posh streets of Rajouri garden. I had known that because I had wandered a fair amount of day the first time I had set out trying to find them. The scent grew stronger for a while and I felt thin sharp blades of ice mulching my brain into porridge.

Suddenly grayness swam over my head and my knees felt weak, as did the possibility of anything around me being real and concrete.

I don't like red roses, its white lavenders or nothing.

For a while, the world didn't make any sense and I didn't realize for a while that I was sweating profusely and was half kneeling beside the front porch.

"It's not real.....doesn't make any sense....I'm not hearing this." I was whispering to myself repeatedly.

Don't like red roses.....white lavenders.....no roses.

The scent faded after a few minutes and I gained a little sanity back to see myself holding the netted steel barricade my father had put up for the little assembly of plants he had grown just outside the house. The upper rim felt smooth and cool in the evening breeze. I stuttered to my feet and turned around to see a boy of six or seven staring at me with a red plastic ball in his hand. I looked at him for a while not sure how to cover up my embarrassing little breakdown in the middle of the alley. I waved uncertainly at the boy and smiled a little. He stood there for a few seconds glancing unapologetically at a grown man behaving like a silly drunk and then off he went, bouncing his red ball down the street.

I dusted off my trousers and stood up straight to regain my composure. *You're just tired, there are no lavenders. No no no, no fucking lavenders.*

I rang the doorbell beside the towering gate, which had been painted black just a few weeks ago. After about four rings and some loud shouts, dad opened the door.

'Are you on leave from the hospital?' he asked on seeing me standing at the door.

"No, dad. I was just worried about you a little and decided to come and see you. Can I come in now?" I said and saw my right shirtsleeve was torn a little from the elbow down.

'What happened there?' he asked pointing to my shirt.

"Nothing, just grazed it somewhere I guess." I replied listlessly.

'Well come on in and give the shirt to me, I'll take care of it.'

"It's all right dad, no need to burden yourself. How are you feeling now, did the pain subside?"

'It's no issue, I'm old and this pain's a part of life now. The earlier one accepts it, the better it behaves.' He said sitting down in front of the television.

'You must be hungry, Shyam has made *kofta* today. It is the one thing he somewhat good at, lousy fellow. Now I'm not that eager to eat as it is, you eat as much as you want.' He said as two politicians abused each other on NDTV news.

"That's okay, I'm not hungry. Just going to take a shower and go to bed."

'Suit yourself; I'll warm it up later if you change your mind.'

"Thanks dad." I said, already halfway up to my room.

I opened the door and the smell of old cardboard and furniture smacked my nose like a dusty old rolled up sheet of newspaper. Although the place was neat and tidy and the bed was covered with new sheets, it reeked of inhabitability. I had not been to my old room for quite a few months by then and it felt a little strange and insecure, somewhat *lonely*. I opened the window to let in fresh air; a little scared by the fact that I might smell lavenders again. *Dirty trick...that's all....the mind plays dirty tricks. Not your fault, the mind's a fucking sadist.* I sat by the window and lit a cigarette. My lips were dry and the cigarette paper stuck between them when I took a light drag. It scathed off some of my lower lip from the inside when I took it out of my mouth. It stung a little, but didn't hurt as much. Nothing did hurt much now anyways. I thought of going over to see maasi but decided against it. I didn't have the energy left to do it. Moreover, there was this other thing where some part of me was a spineless dwarf who didn't have the courage to face her any more.

I took a quick shower and got dressed. The time was quarter to nine. I went down and saw that dad was already asleep on the couch, with the remote in one hand and his dinner plate on the table. I helped him up and took him to his room. I turned on the ceiling fan at full speed and was about to close the door when I heard a faintly spoken '*Radha*' in his sleep. It was my mother's name and this was not the first time I was hearing it in my father's slumber. I came near the bed, folded the bed sheet near his legs and tucked him in. As I turned around to leave, he suddenly clasped my hand with his and I saw that he was wide-awake.

'Sit down, son. I want to talk to you about something.'

I took the chair in front of the study table and sat near the bed, a little surprised by my father's sudden candidness but too tired to think much about it.

'How are you son? I hardly ever see you anymore now.' He asked with such concern that it made me a little shifty in my seat.

"It's the hospital dad, pretty much eats up my whole day. I can shift back here if you need me to." I tried to show concern but my eyes were indifferent to anything happening around me.

'No son, you don't have to do that. And you still haven't answered me....how *are you, really?*'

"I'm fine I guess." I said as I looked down on the floor and started making random shapes with the borders of my slippers.

'It'll pass son, as does every good and bad thing in life. You just have to focus on your work now and not keep thinking about it. Whatever happened has happened. It was not anyone's fault, just like a lightning strike isn't'. He pressed my hand as I sat silently and listened.

'Have you met them recently? You know she calls here sometimes, mostly to ask about you.'

"Not yet Dad, i...I just don't think this is the right time." I tried to hide my cowardice.

'Arjun, tell me honestly. Are you ashamed to face her? Because there's no reason you should be. You tried your best, did you not?'

"I don't know Dad, I don't know what to think about anymore." I said looking down.

'Did I ever tell you about the time I had asked for your mother's hand in marriage?' he asked after a while trying to bring me back from despair.

"No dad, I don't think so." My mind was wandering listlessly.

'Well, it's time you heard it. Might even change your mood.' he raised an eyebrow and elbowed me playfully as I nodded silently.

'I was about thirty two or so at that time and had been appointed as a junior clerk in a small company. I had been seeing your mother for a couple of months by then and, needless to say, she was my world. The day began with her thought and ended with her in my dreams. She was a very pretty girl, not the like the girls nowadays with all their makeup and god knows what. She was simple woman, working in a government college library. You should have seen the crowd in the morning hours of the library, everyone was smitten by her, be it small kids or the town elderly. She had that quality you see, life felt simple around her, even worth living in fact. To this day I can't understand what she saw in me that she agreed to marry me.'

I listened and felt a pang of sadness at that moment. I had no memories of my mother except a few odd dreams and had always imagined how she was in real life. How would she have talked to me, shared her life with me on some sunny days on the terrace and how she would have been here today with me in my utmost moment of anguish, just erasing all the pain with one kiss on the forehead.

'But there was a problem, you see. Your mother was an only child of her folks. Her mother was a very shallow and shrewd sort of woman who hardly ever took notice of anyone below her status and snubbed her nose at everyone. Her father was quite the opposite and I had realized that it could be the only window for a man of my limited means. He had started small and had his own little sweets shop in Rohini that offered the most delicious jalebis you would've ever had in your life. His shop had become quite popular among the neighborhood locals and he had made a decent earning for himself in the process as well. As a man of decent repute and livelihood in those days, his house was constantly flooded with marriage proposals and prospective grooms to be. I waited patiently before going to her parents to ask for her hand in marriage. As soon as I got my first job as junior clerk, I felt it was the right time to make my move.' he said as I saw a little glint in his eyes.

'I got dressed in what I could best muster up with the little I had and rehearsed countless number of times in front of the mirror to get it perfect. I set out for my mission with my head held high and hopes flying in all directions. What I wasn't aware of, was the brewing storm waiting for me. As I sat there in front of her parents with her mother's judging eyes and her father's stern look, my confidence had melted and had piled up in a puddle around my shaking legs.

Her mother spared no expense in humiliating me in every way she possibly could, continuously reminding me of how small a man I actually was in her eyes. I would be lying if I said it didn't feel like a bad movie scene.'

I let out a small laugh and so did dad.

'Her father just sat there and looked at me with big eyes and an impressive looking moustache as I defended myself with whatever little arsenal I had against that witch's army of darkness, who I would have surely set right if she wasn't the mother of my love. But he said nothing. After getting blindsided and coming back to reality, I got up to leave with whatever was left of my dignity and one last glance at your mother who was standing behind the curtains, now teary eyed. I was out the door when her father came from behind and put his arm on my shoulder and said something to me for the first time.'

'Let's take a walk, son.' He said.

'You know you are the first boy in about two years who my wife has shown so much contempt for in the first meeting. She really hates you, but I think I don't have to tell you that, do I?'

'No Sharma ji, it was perfectly clear to me, you don't need to explain.' I said as my mind questioned the purpose of this little rendezvous.

'But it is not her fault, you know. It is very convenient to pass judgment when your own stomach is full, is it not? People like her never shy away from evaluating others as they feel nobody will ever dare to return the favor. She never had to do anything in her petty life, never ever had to cry silently into the night, never had to work through the tears and gulp down the anguish that you and I have had to do, son.' He said looking far off to the trees that had started dancing in the wind.

'I don't understand, Sharma ji.

'You will, in a minute. Did you ever think why I didn't agree to any of the marriage proposals that have been coming day in and day out for the last two years?'

I shook my head silently.

'It is because almost every single person who walks in to marry my daughter, doesn't only want to marry my daughter. They just talk about my shop, how they can help me grow it and pull me in their businesses if they could. They are so foolishly unaware of the beaming greediness and lurch I can see in their eyes. But all that was until this day.'

I looked up at him.

'I can see something in you. You have a certain honesty about you that I have been trying to find in someone for Radha. You have seen the ugly stains of life, and nobody can put a price on that. More importantly, you have a backbone son, not too many around nowadays. It is with you that Radha can truly be happy and content in her life. And not turn out like her mother, that's a little incentive for me.'

'Sharma ji…..I….don't….' *I stuttered with confusion.*

'I am accepting you as a son in law and would be grateful if you would take my daughter Radha's hand in marriage.'

I was dumbfounded by this sudden turn of events and realized I had lost my ability to speak fluently.

'I can't….thank you….enough, uncle.'

'You don't need to do that son. I know my daughter's going to have a better life with you.'

I bent down to touch his feet as a sign of respect and he stopped and embraced me.

I closed the door silently after making sure dad was asleep, reassured that at least someone was close to his share of happiness in life. I opened the microwave and took out the *kofta* bowl. I sat down in front of the T.V and started flipping channels, not giving a shit who got their rights violated or who got elected the biggest douche bag to run the country. The plate of *kofta* in front of me was left untouched as I found myself feeling drowsy and slowly drifting off to sleep.

My dream went back to the fateful night when everything had happened, everything that had blurred my reality made me realize how a simple phone call could derail your life in one instant. *I realized that Destiny, was not without a sense of irony.*

(2)

8th *April 2010, 9.12pm*

The Night when Disaster paid a visit.

"Arjun, Hello? Arjun, where are you right now?" a frenzied voice said at the other end of the line.

"Hello…..maasi? I'm at the hospital right now. What happened? Is everything all right?"

"Arjun…..it's Shreya. She…She…we found her in her room…." She was sobbing uncontrollably.

"Please maasi, calm down and tell me what happened." I prayed to god that it wasn't what I had thought it was.

"We opened her room and she…she was lying in a pool of blood….she cut her wrists, Arjun" I could barely make out what she was saying as she kept crying non-stop and in the background, Mr. Kapoor screaming his daughter's name repeatedly in horror.

For me, it was a moment frozen in time. A moment you remember until the sweet release of death. No matter what shit you go through every day, you can never really prepare for this chapter in the big ugly book of Life. All your maturity, alpha maleness and the sense of calm you force into yourself goes out the window. For some time, the length of which I can't remember, I was just holding a phone and looking out the window into the darkness, not completely myself but still stuck somewhere between reality and a place you sometimes wish you could escape to avoid it. Soon, I was snapped back to reality by some deafening screams.

"Arjun….Arjun….are you there? Please tell us what to do….she is not breathing!"

"Listen to me maasi…..you have to tie something on her wrists to stop the bleeding right now." I said coming back to my senses.

"What….we don't have any bandages at home…what should I do?"

"Just take some cloth or just tear off a *dupatta* or something and wrap it tightly around her wrists, okay?"

"I have tied the *dupatta*…but she's still bleeding Arjun!"

"Take her to Medicare hospital right now….I know someone in the emergency department, I'll inform him and meet you there as soon as possible. Ask for Dr.Amit Saxena on reaching there. There's no time to lose now."

"Okay beta, but please reach as soon as you can."

No sooner did I disconnect the call that I found myself on way to Medicare hospital. I called up, informed Amit, and explained the whole situation. He told me not to worry and said he would handle everything. All through the way, I just kept hoping this was a nightmare and would be over soon.

10.07pm

"Shreya Kapoor please…time of admission around 9.30 pm" I asked frantically on reaching the front nurses desk at Medicare.

"Trauma ICU, third door on the left" said the nurse in a non-chalant fashion after looking up and down her computer screen for a few minutes.

I rushed like hell to the ICU and found Shreya's parents standing outside. Her mom saw me with fresh tears in her eyes. Before I could say anything, she buried her face in my chest and started crying. I held her for a while, not able to say or explain anything. I tried to look at Mr. Kapoor, but he had fixed his gaze towards the floor. I somehow managed to calm her down and made her sit on one of the blue plastic chairs arranged just outside the main ICU entrance.. I searched for Amit inside the ICU and as soon as he caught my gaze, gestured him to meet me outside. I went outside and drank some water to cool my head. As soon as Amit came outside, I caught up with him.

"How is she, Amit?" my voice was beginning to crack.

'It's not looking too good Arjun. When she was brought here, I couldn't get any response from her and her pulse was barely there. Moreover, the cuts were too deep; she might have severed the tendons on her right wrist. She had lost a lot of blood Arjun.'

"Where's she now?" I asked.

'We had managed to stop the bleeding after admitting her to the ICU. She's in surgery right now. It might take a couple of hours.'

"Okay, thanks a lot man. I really don't know what would've happened if you weren't here today." I said as I wiped the sweat off my face.

'Don't worry about it. I bet you would've done the same for me.'

I lit a cigarette and dragged in deep. I offered one to Amit, which he reluctantly declined.

"Since when?" I asked in surprise.

'Ever since the engagement man, I'm not allowed to suck the bud now.'

"Oh that's...great...good for you man." I said as I tried to form proper sentences and took another puff.

'Look Arjun, I'm really sorry about all this. I can't even imagine what you'd be going through right now. But don't kill yourself over it buddy.'

I looked at him with empty eyes and turned my gaze away for a while. I stared silently at the hospital lobby filled with false reassurances and emotionally numb people, all the while thinking the same thing over and over again- *how can I kill myself.....if I I'm already fading away with every second.*

After I went inside, I saw Shreya's father standing near the water cooler. I talked to him and persuaded him to take maasi home, all the while assuring him I would inform them at the earliest about Shreya's condition. After much hesitation and argument, he agreed that it was the best thing to do at the time. I walked both of them outside and opened the car door for her. Just before sitting in the car, she took my hand in both of hers.

"What went wrong Arjun? What did we do wrong? She's been such a good daughter....and you two were so happy together.....how did this happen?" she said as tears rolled down her face.

I kept my hand on her shoulder and said nothing. She sat in the car and they drove away. I kept staring at the taillights until they turned into a blurred mess. I went back inside and had some coffee from the cafeteria on the ground floor. The coffee bitterly burned my throat like a spoonful of hot molten lead. After making my way to the first floor, I started pacing back and forth outside the emergency Surgery Operation Theatre. After a while, I sat down and flicked the plastic cup into the bin. I just sat there with my face held covered by my hands and thought of those words – '*what went wrong Arjun.....what went wrong.....'* echoing through my head. I had known what was wrong but was nowhere near brave enough to tell her that. Sitting there alone with my world crumbling around me, my mind couldn't help but go back to when I could have done something to change the course of things.

(3)

May 4ᵗʰ 2009

Moments with Shreya#1

I had just cleared my Post Graduate Entrance exams and had decided to pay maasi a visit and give her the good news, as it had been a long time since I had last seen her. I had known Shreya's parents since I was about three years old when my father had shifted to Karol Bagh from Rohini where he had procured a job as a local bank employee. My mother had passed away when I was about two and a half years old. *Breast cancer*, my father had told me bluntly, when I had asked him after gathering the nerve to do so in my teen years. It wasn't that my father was an insensitive person; just that I had understood over the years how much my father loved my mother and how much heartache he felt every time anything reminded him of her. Some nights I would see him asleep on the chair holding a framed picture of him and my mother taken in Shimla for their first marriage anniversary. I had never asked him much about her, not because of lack of curiosity about my own mother, but because I just couldn't imagine the pain he must have felt while talking about her. I didn't remember much about my mother other than some things I had gotten to know from my father. He had told me that she was a kind and beautiful woman who really loved and cherished me, rocking me to sleep every night while she sang to me, a sweet little lullaby. I had dreamt of her sometimes, holding me in her arms and caressing my cheeks with her soft hands, but as soon as I would try to reach her face with my little hands, the dream would always fade away.

I had met Shreya's family when my father first moved in the neighborhood and took a house on rent a few blocks away from their home. The rent was cheap and my father was in no mood or condition to keep looking for more options. Shreya's father was the manager of the bank where my father had taken the job and to say the least, was a bit of a disgruntled man. He used to have my father on all fours when he first started at his new job, relentlessly riding him all day long. It wasn't before about a year or so after when my father got his first promotion as junior assistant manager that he relented a little, but I could always feel as though their relationship was a little strained, as if Shreya's father could always feel the presence of a social divide between our families. My father was in every sense of the word, a self-made man and nobody could have argued otherwise. He had started from almost nothing when he had to support his family along with his father in Varanasi by doing minor clerical jobs and other chores, just so that he and my grandparents could eat two meals a day. When he was just twenty years old, my grandfather died of malaria and my dad came to Delhi with my grandmother; supporting the both of them by his own, he had completed his B.Sc from a government college while working at nights as a waiter in a small restaurant. To this day, I always wonder how some men are made of such might.

Unlike her father, Shreya's mother had taken a shining to me as soon as she laid her eyes on me for the first time. And I had to say, the feeling was overwhelmingly mutual. Shreya was an only child the couple had but the decision had not been their own at all. During her second pregnancy, Shreya's mother had to bear a miscarriage and to the couple's lament, her doctor had told them that she could never have another child again. She used to take care of me when my father had to go earn his living during the day. Being the proud man that he was, he wasn't fully supportive of the idea. But being of limited means and seeing Mrs. Kapoor's undeniable fondness for me, he had to give in. As I grew up, somewhere along the way I had started to call her maasi, being completely clueless what that word had actually meant. I guess maybe my innocent ears had caught it flying by to someone's actual aunt. The first time she heard it, she called me to her and sat me up on her lap and asked me if I knew about what I had just said. Being a child of just three or four, the only thought I had was that I had said something awful, and the best thing would be was to look at my feet till I was forgiven. She lifted my chin and kissed me on my cheek. And then, she said something to me. Something I can never forget until this day –

'Arjun beta, do you know what Maasi means? It means **Maa-si** ...*like a mother*. I am like your mother, am I not?

I looked at her and nodded, at the same time suddenly feeling a lump in my throat.

'Do you remember what your mother looked like?' she asked lovingly.

I shook my head and started to feel my eyes welling up with sadness.

She took a little white cloth out of her purse with pink ribbons imprinted on the borders and started wiping my moist eyes.

'Listen Arjun, and always remember this.....you are the most courageous boy in the whole world, there's nothing and nobody who can make you cry ever again. Do you know what your mother told me before going to heaven? She told me that she wants me to take good care of her brave little boy because she loves you just so much, and knows you will grow up to be a very good man one day.' *A sweet lie to an unknowing little child.*

'Now, she has also asked me to make you promise me that you'll never be afraid of anything. It will make her very happy.'

'I promise' I said with the white cloth clenched in hand, my fingers tracing the pink ribbons.

'That's very good Arjun. Do you know that you are a very lucky little boy too? Do you know why?'

I didn't say anything.

'Because not many of us are lucky enough to be loved by two mothers, are we?'

I started sobbing again and put the white cloth on my face. She took the cloth from my hands and hugged me tightly to her chest. Looking back on that day, I honestly feel that those were the few hours for which, I had really slept in all my life. It was almost as if she had filled a big gaping hole in my existence and I filled the little ones in hers.

Shreya's house was like any other old house in Karol Bagh, except that it was in pretty good shape barring the odd creaks here and there. The house was maintained in peak condition owing to renovations being done every few years or so, and the occasional necessary paint job. That's the thing with proud people like Mr. Kapoor- they don't compromise with their houses and cars. The house was a two storey building with a small verandah in the front which housed a little collection of some potted plants-a little leisure pursuit of maasi. Just as Mr. Kapoor had his Stock Market and coin collections, maasi had the company of her green leafy friends. I guess that's the secret of a long happy marriage- that you shouldn't indulge in each other too much after a while. I had bought two big boxes of *mithai* for maasi and it was her favorite too, *kaju barfi*. I loved her too much not to celebrate the occasion in the old-fashioned Indian way. And I had got something for Shreya too, but for a different occasion. It was something that had denied me any moment of slumber for the past few days. I parked my second hand Alto in a small alley in front of the house, walked up to the door and rang the bell. It was midafternoon and my shirt had got a little drenched.

A girl in her teen years answered the door. For a while, I battled with the thought that I had come to the wrong house but the plate stuck beside the door saying Kapoor's settled my nerves.

'Aunty ghar pe hain ya nahi' (Is Aunty there at home or not?) I asked in a typical dilliwallah accent as the girl stared at me waiting for some kind of greeting.

'*Aunty, koi Arjun karke aaya hai*' she turned around and screamed as I mentioned my name, and I fished in my pockets looking around awkwardly at this unexpected welcome.

After a short pause, there was a blunt vocal sound and I recognized it immediately. '*Andar bula lo aur darwaza band karo....machar aate hain*' (*Tell him to come inside and close the door, bloody mosquitoes will come in*). It was Mr.Kapoor, and the reason I recognized his voice was because, he was one of those few people who could make Mother Teresa feel like a terrorist if she ever paid him a visit. I came inside and sat down on the couch a few feet away from him. I put down the boxes of sweets beside me and away from his view. Mr. Kapoor was a diabetic and I didn't want him to think I was going to tease him with them. He did not make any effort to turn his neck away from the television and look at me. I offered him a polite *Namaste* and got a low grunt of acknowledgement in return. *If that's how you want to play it chief, no qualms with me.*

'So, the stock market is going haywire these days, huh uncle?' I said breaking the tearing silence after a while and then realizing what a stupid thing I had just said.

He gave me a look that made me repent my trial at dialogue with him. 'It is as it always is, what's new about it.' He retorted as I felt his eyes scratching the windows of my soul.

'I guess you're right' I said looking very stupid and shifting in my seat. *It is what it is, what the hell was that supposed to mean?*

'Where's *maasi*, uncle?' I asked fully aware he didn't like me calling his wife that, but I had my fun with him every now and then.

He looked at me as if I was an annoying little toddler and gestured towards the kitchen with a sharp jerk of the chin. It looked like the start of an epileptic seizure and I had to bite my lower lip to avoid laughing. I stood up with the boxes of sweets carefully covering them behind my stance and took off for the kitchen.

'Congratulations for your entrance exam.' I heard him say to my back.

'I thought you'd have cleared it last year but, better late than never.' He added with his usual insulting charm.

'Thank you uncle' I said hesitatingly, now a little happy he couldn't savor any of my sweets. *Just shoot me in the balls; you old beaver, if that'll make you happy.*

I made my way towards the kitchen and no sooner had I ducked my head into it, that I was ambushed. The only moment I had was when I saw a glimpse of elation spread across her face. The hug was so tight that I could barely let any air into my lungs. The kisses on the forehead and the stretching of my cheeks to new dimensions didn't cease for a while.

'Maasi, stop it now....I'm not a kid anymore.' I said as I secretly wished for some more warm hugs and bent down to touch her feet.

'*Areyyy*...you are never too old for your maasi.' She said as she pulled my cheeks once again and I pretended to squirm.

'I always knew you'll make it as a big doctor. Didn't I always used to tell you that?' she exclaimed as I tried to hide my inflated chest.

'*Maasi* I just got into the M.D program, it'll be a while for me to become a proper doctor, let alone big.'

'It does not matter, and I am very proud of you today Arjun.' She said with a warm smile that always melted me without fail.

'It's not that big of a deal *maasi*, I just got lucky I guess.'

'*Chup kar*, it's not a small thing, *samjha (Shut up, it's not a small thing you understand?)*. And where have you been for so many weeks, *ab maasi ki yaad nahi aati(Don't you think of your maasi anymore)?'* she asked as I got an unexpected but loving slap on the head.

'I was busy studying *maasi*, it's not like I want to stay away from your exquisite culinary talents.' I said as I opened the box and put a couple of *kaju barfis* in her mouth.

'You remembered? 'She said as she put her hand affectionately on my cheek, the way only a mother can.

'It is not my cooking you miss, is it?' she asked with a mischievous smile on her face.

I tried to look elsewhere but she caught my gaze every time. Finally, I could only manage an embarrassed smile.

'She's in her room upstairs. And she has cooked your favorite dish today too...'

My mouth filled with a tangy sensation and I waited for her to finish her sentence.

'*Kadi-chawal.* It's her special treat for you.' She raised her eyebrows in a playful manner.

'Can I go see her, right now?

'*Arey*, first eat *na*, you must be starving.' She pulled my hand.

'I'll eat in a while *maasi*.....' I said, as I pulled free and stormed upstairs in a hurry.

I had become infatuated with Shreya the first time I had laid eyes on her, or so it seemed each time I had this memory.

I was four and sitting with my father at Ramchand's tea stall playing with a small wooden train model my father had given me on my birthday. It wasn't the most interesting toy in the world, but it was all I had. I had just opened my little pack of cream biscuits and was about to get busy with them, when I saw maasi coming towards us. Only this time, she had a little girl holding her hand. After all these years, I still remember her from that day. A cute little angel in a cute little frock, with her hair in a neatly arranged ponytail tied up with a red ribbon. My biscuits lay on the small wooden table unattended as I found myself staring at the little girl, not knowing what to feel and even if to feel anything. The brain of a four year old can play some goofy tricks; I had come to know that day. As maasi stood at the shop to buy some harvest gold bread and eggs, I could not for the life of me, take my eyes off Shreya. If it wasn't for my inattention of knocking over the toy train and it landing over my little toe, I would've grown old on that chair in that teashop.

'Oooooo.....sssssss...ahhh' I let out a shriek and understood how you never know how heavy a thing can be until it breaks your little toe.

My father saw my shenanigans and scolded me a little followed by a father's reassurance that nothing had happened, but to no avail. My eyes were already wet and I started sobbing in a low hum. Shreya's mother came and consoled me gently, against my father's constant argument that I was okay, that it was nothing. I rubbed my eyes and took my father's hand to leave. As we turned around to go back to our own world, I felt a little pat on my shoulder.

I looked back and saw Shreya holding the toy train, which had intended to butcher my feet.

I stood dumbfounded for a while, not knowing exactly what should have been the right reaction in that situation. When a pretty girl looks at you with big hazel eyes, it doesn't matter how old you are, you'll always find yourself with weak knees. I looked at the train with which I could have deluded myself for months as a source of joy and then I looked at the girl who was sweet enough to bring it *back to me. I took it and looked at it for a few seconds.*

I held out my hand and offered it back to her with an innocent grin.

She took it and gave me a genuine smile that only a child's untainted soul could be capable of, and walked away with the toy in hand. I took my father's hand again and he was surprised to see that his son who had been bawling a few minutes ago had a big smile splattered across his face. I had already forgotten that I had given away my most prized possession to a person I had barely known then.

As we grew up, my affections for her had also grown stronger. I couldn't have said the same about her though. She was like a free soul and friendly with everyone, that was the thing that I had hated the most about her. To ignore someone is acceptable to a certain degree, but treating them like everybody else seemed quite cringe worthy. Even if she had thought of me in an affectionate manner, she never showed it much and I couldn't read her mind either. She had opted for a Biotechnology course in Dehradun and it was the saddest news for me at that time. We used to talk once or twice a week at nights, when she used to go up to the roof in the mid-January chill so that she could catch the signal clearly. We were friends, this was the only thing I was sure of, and it wasn't until my third year in medical college, that I finally gathered enough courage to tell her how I felt about her. *That was a sure bummer*, I thought of that episode as I made my way up to her room.

The door was already half open as I peeked in quietly and saw her head deep into her cupboard of stacked clothes, which had seemed like a constantly dividing colony of bacteria every time I saw it. I moved in slowly and hugged her from behind, the smell of her hair blinding my senses and my lips enjoying the soft experience of her neck. She wasn't startled a bit and kept busy rearranging her vicious load of clothes.

'I told you *Sanjay*, I have a boyfriend now....*we can't keep doing this you know.*' She said keeping one hand on the side of my neck and sounding a little flirtatious and playful.

I felt my heart suddenly pounding in my chest as I backed up my steps and chose to ignore the foot of the dresser that had sat just behind the closet. I tripped and fell, my rear end taking the full brunt of the fall and the box of *kaju barfi* falling on the bed that had already been occupied by a large family of teddy bears and countless soft pillows. She turned around and saw the expression on my face, which was like that of a man who caught his wife cheating in his own bed. She let out a jovial laugh.

'And you thought you would surprise me.' She said and winked.

'Don't ever do that again Shreya, *got it?* It's not funny, okay.' I said as I got up and rubbed my sore behind.

'*Awww......*' she said in her typical teasing manner. 'You have to say, it is definitely a little funny, you look like a stock market investor who just lost all his money.' She said as she came towards me and the sweet aroma of white lavenders flirted with my nostrils. I was dusting off my clothes when she came near me and kissed me on the cheek.

'You sure Sanjay won't mind?' I teased her back with a hint of sarcasm.

'You men are worse than children at jealousy. Do you even know a Sanjay who lives around here?' she said as she put her hands on her waist to make a point. 'And even if he did mind, it wouldn't stop me from making out with my boyfriend now, would it?'

'Is that so?' I asked, now seeing her properly for the first time in months. She had worn a white T-shirt with a little kitten playing with a fur ball on it and jeans which were torn at the kneecaps. It was an unbelievably sexy sight for me and it felt like a rainstorm plundering through a barren steaming desert. I realized only at that moment how long it had been since I had seen her, *seen the love of my life.*

'Come here you silly boy.' She said as she wrapped her arms around my neck and I got a warm feeling in my belly. 'I missed you so much, stupid' she whispered in my ear and ruffled my hair from behind.

My heart became overcome with such unexpected elation that I had trouble finding any words for a few seconds. I had always known the fact that I loved Shreya more than anything else in the whole world; but at that moment, wrapped in her warm embrace and feeling her soft body against my palms, I knew there could be no other person, ever in this world, who would ever take her place. I realized the strangeness of the thought but ignored it. *I could not have loved her more.*

'I missed you too, like hell.' Was all I could whisper back in her ears and thought I heard a quiet sniff.

I pulled her away against my mind telling me not to, and saw that her eyes had become moist and the reflection of the fluorescent white light in the room shone like sparkling little diamonds in them. *It was a remarkable sight.*

'What's wrong?' I asked, now a little concerned.

She looked at me with her big hazel eyes and gave me a playful pat on the cheek. 'Nothing's wrong *paagal*...just haven't seen you for so long, the months feel like decades.'

'Yeah, tell me about it.' I didn't say much else as I realized it was written clearly on my face that I had felt the same way, *maybe more.*

'*Oh!* I almost forgot. Congratulations, Mr. Big Shot Doctor for finally making it big!' She said as she tried to pull my cheeks and I imagined them screaming- *please, no more.....no more, we'll do anything but please no more for today.*

'It's Doctor Big Shot now, and he doesn't like getting his cheeks pulled at all.' I said as I moved to the side and grabbed her soft cheeks instead.

'*Owwww*…you dog. Don't pull so hard.' She screamed as I let go of her silky smooth cheeks.

'I can't help it…..*you're cho chweet.*' I mimicked a cartoon like voice and she gave me a million dollar smile.

She picked up the *kaju barfi* from the bed and stuffed her mouth with a couple of pieces. *The Fondness for dairy sweets runs in the family, I guess.* I reached over and tried to take a piece but she slapped my hand away. 'This is for me Dr.Arjun…you will not be getting any sugar today.' she smiled playfully.

'The joke's on you, *sally*. I already shared a couple of them with *maasi*.' I used to call her *sally* sometimes to prick her nerves. It had first started when we had watched *When harry met Sally* for the first time on HBO and she had started crying during the scene when he finally proposes to sally by giving a really corny speech. Since then, I had never missed an opportunity to tease her about it, much to her annoyance.

'*Ha ha ha,* so funny Dr.Wise-ass. Why don't you go down and spend more time with her.

God knows she's more of a mother to you than she's ever been to me.' She said tossing the box in front of the mirror on the dresser.

'Hey, cut me some slack, okay. I didn't have my own mom around like you did. And she does not love me more than you, okay.' I tried to look dejected.

She looked at me with her head cocked to one side and her stare directly locked into my eyes.

'Okay fine, maybe she does. But you can't *really* blame her, who *can* resist my charms?

'Don't dream so bright in the day, Dr.Arjun. She won't be so thrilled when I tell her that you used to have an affair with the smoky bud. ' she said coolly and was pleasantly satisfied on seeing the look of unadulterated horror on my face.

'Yeah, right. You had better not do that miss. Anyway, I don't smoke anymore, and she probably won't even believe it.' I tried to sound in control of the situation. 'So what's up with your old man, he looks at me every time as if I've just come in after a rampage of serial killings.' I said as she laughed and seeing her, I myself broke into a smile.

'I don't know. He the girl's dad after all, you know. Maybe he doesn't trust your intentions with me.' She said raising an eyebrow.

'Oh really, is that it? Then I can't really blame him, he's not wrong in his thought process. My intentions are never good around you.' I said and followed it with a naughty smile.

'Oh don't worry, that's not news to me.' She said, still laughing and looking swell doing it.

'It's just his diabetes, I guess. He doesn't say much about it but I know it's on his mind all the time. I tried talking to him a couple of times, but he just fends it off. Poor dad, he's such a sweet guy.'

'Yes, definitely as sweet as a sour lemon. I wonder how sour people can get diabetes.' I couldn't help joking as Shreya punched me on the shoulder and my arm abused me for infuriating her.

'Okay okay sorry, I didn't mean it.' I said hoping it would stop the abuse on my arm.

After she had calmed down and was smiling again, I walked to the door and closed it gently. I took her hand in mine and looked at her lovingly. I made her sit down on her bed beside me and gazed into her big beautiful eyes.

'Shreya, I love you more than anything. I hope you know that.' I said holding her soft hands in mine.

She seemed a little flushed by the sudden change in the subtlety of the room but maintained her composure. 'You know I do, Arjun.' She said as she pressed my hand a little.

'Well, there's been this thing on my mind for some time now and I can't hold out much longer.' I said and saw her expression change into a more serious one.

'I have something for you, Shreya.' I said as I took a little blue box from my right pocket, my eyes still guarding the periphery where the door stood and my ears on the lookout for the sound of footsteps. I bent down near the bed on my knee and took her hand in mine, flipping open the box with the thumb of my left hand. I tried to match her gaze which was firmly fixed on the small round thing in the blue box, which had set her lazy afternoon into a roller coaster; her lips trying their best to stop quivering and cover the distance between themselves. She finally looked at me with those big eyes that had started experiencing some drizzle on a hot Tuesday afternoon. *Girls cry at almost anything, it's surely an extra-ordinary gift.*

'Shreya Kapoor, you are the love of my life. I don't know how you feel about me, but for me you are the air I breathe and the wind I feel every day. You are my morning, my dawn, anything, and everything in between when the sun and the moon dance around the horizon. Not a single second of my life goes by, when I'm not thinking of you. Not thinking of your beautiful eyes, your pink lips or the way you look when you're trying to figure out something, with your hands on your leaning head as you look far into the distance. *It had begun to feel really cheesy in my head but it would look awfully stupid if I had stopped then.*

When I'm awake, I dream about you and when I sleep, you are my reality. I love your kindness and the way you never think twice about your decisions. I feel as lucky as the desert prophet who finds an oasis, to have you in my life. *You are my oasis, Shreya.* Every moment I spend with you is one beautiful dream, but it's even better than that as I can cherish it without the fear of waking up at any second. All I can honestly say is that I can live without any air in my lungs or water down my throat, but I *cannot* live without you in my life. But my biggest regret is that I could never fall in love with you, because you can't fall in love with the person you've loved your whole life. And I promise you that I'll love you till the end of my days and beyond, you'll see.' *Okay kid, it's the final lap, time for the big finish.* 'So, in the end of this boring speech, all I want to ask you is – Shreya Kapoor, *will you do me the honor of marrying me and be the nagging wife I've always wanted you to be?'* my heart pounded so hard that I had to keep my hands from bouncing up and down.

I had poured my heart out and it felt good that the speech that I had been trying to cram had finally gone smoothly, but it also felt like I had shed my clothes and was standing naked on the highway, *I felt completely vulnerable.* I looked at her, now clasping my hand firmly and her lips escaping a small quiver. My eyes and ears had stopped paying any attention to the door and along with my other senses, were engrossed in anticipation. I noticed my right hand was on the verge of a tremor.

She looked pensive, as if negotiating a nuclear treaty between India and Pakistan, being ever so careful not to falter in her decision. She stole her eyes from the ring and looked at me.

'You think I'll be a nagging wife? She finally said with a smile that set right my jittering nerves.

I looked at her, not knowing what to say after what was, according to me, a damn good proposal and must've looked somewhat mixed up.

'Yes, of course I'll marry you stupid, I love you so much.' She screamed as my fear of her sound reaching her dad downstairs came roaring back. I put the ring on her finger and hugged her.

'That was a beautiful speech, Arjun. Never would have expected this from you'. She said in my ear as I pretended it was nothing, *just in a day's work.* She was looking at the ring again.

'I know it's not much but it's the best I could afford right now.' She gave me a look that threatened to blow my head into a million pieces as if to say - *I'll kill you if you ever say that again.*

'I want to marry you, not the ring.' She said and nudged my head with her fingers.

'Shit, sorry. But you can't tell your folks about this right now, not even *maasi.*' I said as I came back to my senses and candy land faded away. 'Not a word.'

'What? Why so?' she said as a wave of disappointment spread across her face.

'It's not the right time Shreya. We'll wait until your graduation; it's in a couple of months, right? I've already talked to dad about it. He'll talk to your old man after you graduate.'

'Is it really necessary?' she asked studying her hand for the millionth time.

'Yes, it has to be our little secret for some time.' I said as I lost myself in her sparkling eyes again.

'So, Dr. Arjun, you finally have me now. Good job trapping me.' She said with a sly smile.

'You shouldn't have taken my *toy train* then.' I said and we both laughed.

I was brought back to her room and my senses by the shouts of the young teenage girl from downstairs.

'*Didi,* come down for lunch, it is getting cold.' Her screams were followed soon after by maasi's.

'I looked at Shreya and saw her lost in her own little world and smiling. I shook her a little and told

72

her to keep the ring with her until my father makes it official with hers. I walked towards the door with Shreya's hand in mine and put my hand out to open it.

'Hey, I think I forgot something.' I said as Shreya shrugged and rolled her eyes.

'What? I don't see anything.' She said looking around.

'This.' I said as I put my hand on her waist and pulled her towards me. With my eyes locked into hers and ours heartbeats synchronizing into one, I kissed her on the lips, relishing the soothing warmth of her body against mine.

(4)

June 17ᵗʰ 2006

Moments with Shreya#2

The First Proposal

It was the summer of 2006 and I had gone to Shreya's house to pick her up for a movie and dinner as she had come home for the holidays. I had come fully prepared for the occasion, wearing a white cuffed shirt and dark brown trousers and a bouquet of a dozen white lavenders in hand. I rang the doorbell and she answered the door in a blue t-shirt and jeans.

'Hey, what's the occasion?' she said trying to be funny.

'Nothing, can't I look nice and decent sometimes?' I retorted and gave her the flowers.

'Okay okay, I was just kidding around. You look very handsome. And thank you, these are lovely.'

'Thanks. You ready to go?' I said looking at my watch.

'Sure, I'll just be back in a few seconds.' She said as she ran off inside.

I looked at my watch as the seconds turned to minutes and I began to feel like a flower delivery guy who took his job a bit too seriously so as to dress up for it. I had made dinner reservations at the Primrose restaurant, which was the classiest place in Karol Bagh at the time; although I had known, it would cost me an arm and leg. Finally, she came out after fifteen minutes or so and we were on our way.

'So which movie are we seeing?' she asked in the car.

'I thought first we'll have something to eat and then see the movie, any one you want.' I said and cautiously waited for her reply.

'Okay, that's cool. Where are we going then?'

'It's a surprise.' I said as she raised her eyebrows but said nothing.

I parked the car near the restaurant and opened the raggedy door of the Alto for her. She got out and stood there, a little confused.

'This way.' I said with a direction of the hand.

She saw the restaurant and seemed a little surprised. 'Well, looks like somebody's in a generous mood today.' She said poking her elbow into my gut.

'Nothing like that. It's just a nice place to spend some time.' I said as I opened the entrance door for her.

We sat down at our reserved table as the neatly dressed waiter smiled politely and presented us our menus. I opened the card and tried to stop my heart from going into a flutter after seeing the prices. But the prices didn't matter; I had to do what I had come there to do. We placed our orders and made a little small talk in between the awkward smiles. I gathered all my little courage, which had formed a lump in my throat as she sipped her drink silently.

'Shreya, I wanted to talk to you about something.' I said as she looked at me with the straw still in her mouth. She left it in the drink and stared at me, giving me her full attention.

'You know we've known each other for quite a while now, I mean sixteen years is no small time to get to know someone. And I have a lot going on in my life right now, mostly good stuff and I feel settled somewhat. I don't know about you but I feel we can finally be more than friends now.'

As I said this, the waiter brought our orders and settled them on the table, chicken fried rice for me, and shahi paneer with roti for her. I didn't notice his smile this time around, as my gaze was firmly planted on Shreya and I noticed her expression had turned into a fairly shocked one. That made me hesitate a little but I was already in mid ocean.

'What I'm trying to say is......I'm crazy about you Shreya, I always have been and I would have cursed myself my whole life if I hadn't told you this.'

She looked at me as if realizing why I had brought her to that restaurant and I could see the look of being flabbergasted on her face.

'Arjun, I...don't think this is the right time for me to be in a relationship.' She said looking at her plate after a few seconds and shifted in her seat a little.

'What do you mean? I felt myself choking up.

'I just think this can wait, you know. I haven't been with anybody else and you haven't either, don't you think we should have some options at this point?'

she said supposedly terrified that I may have a fit of rage or a breakdown there and then.

'I mean, there's a whole world out there, you know. So many things to do, to experience, in so little time. I just want to see what's out there Arjun; feel the rush of independence for the first time in my life. I want to see what I can be and do on my own, without any boundaries. Don't you?' she said with the blood rush filling her cheeks as I looked on, amazed and somewhat terrified at her thrill.

'Umm…I guess you're right. When you're right, you're right.' I was in too much pain to realize that I was saying right over and over again. But I maintained my composure. I took out what I had in my right pocket and sat it on the table. It was a beautiful Silver Titan watch, with Shreya's name engraved on the flipside. I had got it for her as a gift, but now it looked and felt like an eyesore. I was sure if I had brought it back home with me that night, it wouldn't have seen the light of day again.

'Here, I got this for you.' I said not looking at her.

'Why?' she asked.

I looked at her with a curt expression, not because I wanted to hurt her but just because my own hurt was having trouble keeping down its ugly head.

'Oh sorry, stupid question.' She said as she opened the box.

'It's really lovely Arjun.' She said as she felt her engraved name with her fingers and I felt the dire stab of ingratitude. "It's lovely"? Ya, right. I spend the whole damn afternoon in boiling heat just to find the place where they do this shit and all I get is "lovely". *A big dump on my day is what it is.*

'It's not as beautiful as you are, but I tried my best.' I said silently as she gave me a look that probably said – It is beautiful but I'm just not interested in it or you.

'I can't take this Arjun, it looks a little pricey.' She wasn't wrong about the 'pricey' part but was about the 'little' part. I had saved money for two years to buy her that eyesore of a watch that now told me my time was up.

'If you don't like it, throw it in the dustbin or something.' I said, now really feeling hurt and I felt she sensed it too.

'Don't say that Arjun, I really love it. Thank you for this gift.' She said and kept it inside her purse.

We spent the rest of the evening in silence, more or less. She ate her food quietly while I stared at mine wondering if I could ever swallow solid food again. We made a little small talk about insignificant things and I finally gestured the waiter to end my agony. He brought the bill and I gave him my card as he spotted my plate, which was still full of rice and chicken.

'Something wrong with the food sir?' he asked with fake concern.

I looked at him as if to say "Yes, something's definitely wrong with the food, it's terribly unlucky for me, I just got fucked". I decided against saying anything and asked him if he could please hurry up the proceedings so that I could take this embarrassment elsewhere. We walked back to the car and I started the engine. The whole time back to her house was a silent blur as neither one of us was sure of anything to say. As I stopped the car in front of her house, she got out and stood outside the car.

'Can I just say something?' she said after twiddling her fingers on the window for a while as I sat behind the wheel, unsure of what to do next in my life. The world had begun to seem more cruel and darker than it already was.

'I think you've said enough.' I said curtly, not caring how much it hurt her.

'Arjun, Please try to…' she was left hanging as I put the car in gear and drove off. I looked back in the rear view mirror and saw her still standing there and looking at the back of my car, stranded in her thoughts.

(5)

25ᵗʰ October 2009

Moments with Shreya#3

A few months after Shreya'sGraduation.

A few months working in the Medicine department and I had scratched and banged my head from wall to wall. I could not remember the last time I had slept peacefully for a couple of hours. I had lost a lot of weight and my face was a constantly changing canvas of tiredness, anxiety and irritation. Each day began in a daze and ended just the same. Sometimes it had begun to feel like a really wrong and horrible life choice; as the eternal abuses from my senior consultants and the workload dump from my seniors had become a harsh routine in my days. I would have been lying if I had said I didn't get an intense craving to light a cigarette during some of those days. Every time I used to see someone pulling a fag (and believe me, you start seeing more and more when you quit), a small voice inside me said *just take one, you'll feel better I promise. Look what you've done to yourself; don't you want to feel better?* But somehow, I would manage to shut that voice out. I had been so sunken in my daily schedule that I had not been able to make it to Shreya's graduation function and she was somewhat pissed about it. We had gotten engaged just after her graduation (it was a surprise to me how easy it was, considering how her old man looked at me with such visual stench, but my father had said that's how a girl's father is, it wasn't his fault), and the family had let us decide about the date of marriage. 'We'll talk about it later' Shreya had said a few days after we got engaged. I had found a house nearby the hospital and set it up with Vibhor to share the rent, as the daily traffic was killing me and more over, I had round the clock duties about half the month. One day I had got a call from Shreya asking me (mostly telling me) if I could meet her at the earliest, that she wanted to talk to me about something. I looked at my duty roster and winced in mental agony. 'Let me clear something up, *babe*' I had told her. I shuffled around my duties with my Co-pgs and finally got the day off somehow. As I was leaving the hospital, my inner voice broke its slumber again - *From 'I'll love you till the end of my days' to 'let me clear something up'*, boy this girl is sure lucky to have you in her life.

I had told Shreya that I would meet her up around seven at her house. I reached home at about six thirty and decided to wash up a little to clear my head and then go over to Shreya's place. The evening light was fading away like a volatile dream and the crickets had started their night charades. As I stopped the car and got out with my stethoscope hanging around my aching neck and a dirty apron hanging over my shoulder, I saw Shreya sitting on the front porch. She was wearing a white top and a long red skirt. She had her hands clasped together and they were having a conversation with her mouth. I dragged my lifeless body towards the house, with my head aching and eyes begging to be closed shut. Shreya saw me when I opened the main gate to get in and gave me a brief smile. I tried to offer her one, but it felt like I had forgot how to do it.

I kept my bag and other stuff on the welcome mat and sat down beside her on the porch. Only after I had sat down, I realized my legs felt like a couple of stiff bamboo shoots. I stretched them out and crossed them across the hardwood floor. After we sat there silently for a couple of minutes, I finally spoke just to avoid falling unconscious.

'You're looking very pretty today.' I said stating what was an obvious fact for me and then realizing that she actually looked serene in the blue evening glow of the moon.

'You carry that lavender scent everywhere, it's amazing.' She smiled a little, as I smelled her hair.

'Thanks.' she finally said looking at my tired face, which got a small shot of life when it saw her smile.

'Are you okay, *babe*? You look a little worried.' I said trying my best to stay awake and put my arm around her shoulder and rubbed it a little.

'Have you ever thought why the sun looks *orange* just before it sets, Arjun?' she asked out of the blue, staring right into my eyes.

'What kind of question is that? Why do you ask?' I counter questioned, too hazy to act surprised, but she just looked on.

'Well, I guess it's nearer to the horizon as it sets, not too sure though.' I said not actually knowing the answer and just cutting some bullshit.

She looked far and beyond for a few seconds and turned her gaze towards me again. 'Forget that I asked. How've you been? You look beat up.'

She asked with genuine concern.

'Thanks for the sweet compliment, *my love*.' I said and it brought back that smile I could die a million deaths for. 'It's just work, you know. And I'm *really* sorry I couldn't come to your graduation; I really wanted to, you know.'

'It's okay, no worries. At least I got to see you today after two months you went missing. I don't care about some stupid graduation.' She said as she stroked my hair and it felt good.

'I really missed you Shreya.'

'I know.' She said and stared at the porch for a while.

'I wanted to ask you for some advice, it's for a *friend*. You remember Aashita, don't you? She said signaling my ears to return to function.

'Yeah, you've mentioned her, a couple of times.' I said groggily.

'Well it's about her. She found out she's pregnant a few days ago.' She said running her fingers through her hair with one hand sending frizzled vapors of her scent towards me.

'And I guess she's not married yet, and that's the issue here?' I asked patiently.

'No, she's not and she's very scared. I know she can be a little *overfriendly* with guys at times but this news was a shocker, even to me.'

'So, has she decided anything about this?'

'She asked me what to do when she first found out, but I had no reply. I consoled her and told her that I would help her sort things out this weekend. I don't know what to say to her, *I really don't*. What do you think?'

I studied her face for a few moments before saying anything. It was a little pale now as if the situation had deeply affected her somehow. *How I wish to this day that I should have just asked her what was really wrong, what was really eating her up from the inside. How I wish I could have those few seconds back and realized that this was not just great concern for a friend, but more. How I should have jolted my tired brain into action, just for those few moments, only if I had.*

'I think she should have an abortion as soon as she can.' I said more bluntly than I had intended to.

She looked at me with protesting eyes. 'How can you say it like that?' she reacted, just short of being furious.

'Well, what do you want me to say? It's the best option for her right now, Shreya.' I protested with the little strength I had left.

'How can you not think about her, about what *she's* going through at this time? Don't you feelanything for anyone but yourself?' She was yelling now.

'What? Where did that come from? I was just trying to help you and your friend out here, it's not like I'm going to have something come out of it.' I was fuming.

'You don't have to be a jerk about it, just think about how she might feel about this; killing a child, taking a life.'

I can't remember if it was the throbbing headache or my overflowing brain reaching up to my ears at that time but right then I said something so utterly horrible and despicable that it still haunts me like a stench of torrid memory on some days. How naive I was back then, was beyond recognition.

'Look it doesn't matter how I feel about it, but I know for sure that kid won't feel good being called a bastard for the rest of his life!'

As I finished this sentence, I saw anger bubbling up in her eyes and heard a definitive *Whapp!*, a few seconds later. She had slapped me hard across the face that had just landed me short of seeing the Looney toons flying around my head in circles. I felt my left cheek burning up into a flaming red sensation. Shreya had covered her face with her hands and was crying badly. I didn't know whether to nurse my screaming cheek or to console my sobbing girlfriend. Being a little cautious, not to get a high five on the face again, I put my arm around her and she tilted her head to rest on my shoulder.

'I'm honestly sorry, *babe.* I shouldn't have said those words. I don't know what came over me; you know I'm so stupid sometimes. Hey come on, please stop crying, I'm really sorry about it.' I tried to make my case.

'It's okay. I'm sorry too; I shouldn't have slapped you *so hard.*' She said after she had stopped crying a bit and had put her soft hand on my inflamed cheek.

'Oh, it's nothing; I'm used to more at work.' I said and it made her giggle a little.

I saw her glistening face in the moonlight and she looked as beautiful as I had ever seen her. I cursed myself for making the girl I had loved so much, cry. I looked deeply into her eyes for a while and was about to say something when she stopped me abruptly.

'Don't say it…I already know what you want to say.' she said with beaming clarity.

I put both my hands on her cheeks and kissed her forehead. I came closer to give her a hug and whispered in her ears, that I loved her.

'Tell you what, how about we talk about this in a few days? I promise I'll take a much-needed leave and we'll have the whole day to talk, okay *babe*?'

Sometimes when alone, I used to think of this moment and imagined myself going back in time and kicking my past self in the nuts, and saying – *Don't let her go, you idiot. Wake up and talk to her now, or you'll lose her forever.*

She agreed and wiped her eyes with my handkerchief. I walked her home and she kissed me on the cheek when we reached the door. I waved goodbye and went home tired and half-asleep. As I passed the front porch, something shiny caught my eye. I took a closer look and saw, that it was the engagement ring I had given to Shreya, and it was laying there like an unclaimed piece of junk on the dusty porch. I picked it up and looked at it.

'Must've dropped it by mistake.' I said to myself; too beat up to realize the simple fact that *nobody drops an engagement ring on the ground, no no, not at all.* I went inside and crashed on the couch in the living room.

Little did I realize that, we were never going to talk about it ever again. In fact, she never even mentioned it a second time. As the months passed, she seemed to move on and so did I, until she decided to cut herself seven months later and move me closer to insanity than anything else ever could.

(6)

Back to that fateful night.

9ᵗʰ April 2010, 1.30 Am

My final moments with Shreya.

I had fallen asleep sitting outside the Surgery OT, hoping and waiting for the Surgeon to come out and tell me everything's all right, *no worries at all*. I was woken up by a shake of the shoulder and saw it was a tall man with a green cap and a facemask. My eyes burned as I rubbed them to reality.

'Arjun Vashisht?' he asked in a husky voice.

'Yes?' I enquired.

'Hello, I am Dr. Subroto Banerjee. I couldn't meet you before starting the surgery but it's done now.' He said with an expression so calm and unattached that it was almost soothing. I shook his hands and introduced myself.

'How is she now, *sir*?' I asked, trembling from the inside.

'Come into my room Mr. Vashisht and we'll talk.' He said like a man in charge and I just nodded.

We sat down in his room and for the first time that night, I felt the cool breeze from the Air Conditioner rippling through my sweaty shirt and it felt good. He ordered some tea for himself and asked me what I would like to drink. I politely declined and asked about Shreya.

'Well, it is a dicey situation, Mr. Vashisht....'

'Please, call me Arjun.' I said interrupting him.

'Okay, Arjun. As I said, the situation is not as ideal as we would want it to be. She had lost quite a lot of blood when we had started to operate on her, and her vital signs were bleak. But we repaired the torn tendons and the arteries, and gave her two units of blood during the procedure.' He said carefully demonstrating with his hands as I patiently listened as if I were a five year old.

'We were lucky enough that her vitals came back and are maintaining pretty good shape right now *but...*' he stopped for a few seconds and I knew the reason.

'You're worried about Hypovolemic shock, isn't it?' I said finally.

'Yes, Arjun. Losing so much blood so quickly can cause the body organs to shut down at any time in the first twenty four hours, but I don't need to tell you all this, do I?'

'I understand.' I said blankly.

'We'll shift her to a private ICU room down the hall and monitor her carefully for the night. She seems stable now but has to make it through tonight. If anything can go wrong, it will most probably during the next ten or twelve hours.'

I began to curse myself for knowing so much about the perils of blood loss. I had seen so many cases of traffic accidents and monitored so many, it was hard for me to be optimistic at the time.

'But, let's not lose hope now. *She* needs it the most.' He said as I paid my sincere gratitude and we shook hands again.

I followed the ward boy as he shifted Shreya's bed trolley into the Private ICU unit and helped him set up the apparatus there. As he was about to draw the blood samples, I hesitated a bit and stopped him. 'I'll do it.' I said to him and sank the sharp steel into the veins of the girl who had made my life worth living. *I'm sorry my love, I'm hurting you for the very last time.*

After he had gone with the samples, I was alone with Shreya for the first time during that dreadful night. I took a seat beside her bed and looking at her at that moment, I realized how alone I felt. It didn't feel like sadness, but seeing her lying unconscious, wrapped in tubes and bandaged wrists, I felt a sense of deep depression taking over me and enclosing me from all corners in my life. I already felt she had left me and I had nowhere to go, nothing to do now. It was a strange thought, that nothing would be the same anymore, nothing would matter after her. It was as if time had refused to move on and stood still; mocking me, mocking my erroneous ways. It seemed like a final chapter in my life or for that matter, the end of my world, as it had existed once. *Melancholy, it had seemed to be. Knowing that doom just lay around the corner when everyone else is busy thinking it wasn't. There would be no hope after her, just a vacant cave of what had once been a garden of germinating dreams.*

I caressed the hair off her face and took her hand in both of mine. *'Why'd you do it, Shreya? Why? Why didn't you just leave me and find somebody better than me? Somebody who truly deserved you. Somebody who understood that you are invaluable in every way, somebody who had known better and protected you from this evil wretched world'* I thought to myself as I held her hand to my lips.

'Please wake up and call me stupid again. I'll do anything to hear those words from you. Slap me, punch me in the face or just hit me wherever you want. Just please wake up Shreya.' I begged her as neither she nor the empty room gave me an answer.

I closed my eyes for a few minutes, which felt like decades. After an hour or so, I felt her fingers slightly moving and pressing my hand. I opened my eyes and saw her eyes open halfway and wandering slowly around the room. Finally, she caught my gaze.

'Hey *babe*, welcome back. Thought I lost you there for a while.' I said as I kissed her hand.

She tried to smile but could only afford a slight lift in her face. She looked as beautiful as she always had been to me. I saw her take a little swallow and asked if she wanted water. I removed her facemask for a couple of seconds and put the glass to her mouth, with one hand behind her neck supporting it. She could not move her right hand much as the tendons were cut too deep. I took the glass of water and kissed her forehead.

'I missed you, *babe*. You look beautiful, by the way.' I said holding her right hand in my palms.

She tried to smile again and it gave me a little ray of illuminant joy. She moved her right hand away from my hands and kept it on my right cheek, wincing with each movement. She felt it a little with her fingers and tried to pull it, but her battered body would not allow it. I smiled at her and felt her forearm with my hands. It wasn't as warm as I was used to and it gave me a ghastly feeling. *I prayed to God my worst enemy wouldn't have to endure the suffering that I was going through.*

'Shreya, I .....' I was about to say something when she weakly put her finger on my lips and mover her head from side to side. I tried to hold her hand but she wouldn't let me. I did not know what she wanted. She put her finger on the bed sheet and started making a sign I couldn't understand at first. I knew she wanted to tell me something, something important, as she didn't seem drowsy at all now. I tried to comprehend the alphabets she made on the sheet with her weak fingers – J-O-U-……..

…-R-N-…….

…A…..L.

'Journal? Is it a journal?' I asked her and she nodded seeming satisfied.

'What journal?' I asked her confusingly and saw her in agony of not being able to make me understand.

She opened her mouth and gestured at me to remove the oxygen mask so she could speak. I told her not to tire herself but she would not listen. She kept gesturing me by her hand to do so and finally, I relented. I took off the mask and she grabbed me close as I bent down, until I could hear her breaths oscillating my eardrums. She choked inside her own voice while trying to speak.

'Jour….journal……under….the   train.'   she whispered with her tired breath and let go of my shirt.

I put on her oxygen mask again and sat down. 'There's a Journal under a train?' I repeated to her and she nodded weakly.

'Okay, I understand.' I said to make her feel comfortable. The truth was however, I had not understood anything about that sentence, but wanted her to believe me just the same. I did not want her to be in any more agony because of me.

'You should get some sleep now.' I said to her, knowing that every bit of energy she spent was a poison arrow into her heart.

She didn't try to protest this time, just looked at me, worn out and exhausted.

'I love you, Shreya...' I said as I bent near her cheek and kissed her cold cheek one last time '.....and don't you ever forget it even for a second.'

I saw her face, which had curled up into a smile and I realized, just in that split second that our eyes met, *both of us were seeing each other die slowly.*

I went and sat outside the room for a little while, with an sinister thought brewing inside my head that I had seen her for the last time. I ignored it but it kept coming back. Thankfully, to distract me, there was a picture on the wall opposite me showing a father holding hands with his son while both of them walked through a yellow forest. The tagline had read-

MY FATHER NEVER TAUGHT ME HOW TO LIVE,

HE JUST LIVED, AND LET ME WATCH HIM DO IT.

I suddenly wished my father had taught me how to deal with this situation or maybe I could have watched him take care of my mother when she was dying of Cancer. I kept looking at the poster with my hands intermingled and mind nowhere to be found. As I was lost in my thoughts, I felt a tap on my shoulder. It was Amit, who had come to check up on me after the surgery.

'Hey, how is she?'

'She's hanging on, what else can I say?' I said as I felt I had no expressions left on my face any more.

'Get some sleep bro, you look like hell.' He said with his hand on my shoulder.

100

'I'm okay here.' I said. 'She needs me to be with her'.

'Look I've got the best nursing staff available for monitoring her. Get a couple of hours sleep in the duty room and I'll wake you up myself if anything happens, okay?'

I hesitated a lot but I knew I was an engine running without any fuel; I did not have any ounce of strength left in my body. I finally agreed and made sure he would come and get me, even for the smallest turn of events. I saw Shreya once more through the window, sleeping serenely, and went away to get some shut-eye.

The dream had started like a tranquil rainbow after a mild rain shower. I saw myself in a beautiful garden filled with white and blue lavenders, their scent filling my lungs with life. Far off into the garden, I saw Shreya sitting below a tree playing with something in her hands. As I went nearer, I saw that she had a little wooden toy train in her hands and was looking at it curiously. I was suddenly happy, too happy to even describe it. I started walking near her and called out her name, which seemed to come from a far distance all around me. But she didn't listen. I came nearer and called her again, but she was too involved with the toy in her hands and paid no attention to me. 'She must still be upset with me', I thought. Suddenly, she looked at me, but not in a loving or affectionate way. It was a look of sudden terror and fright. I moved towards her to tell her that it was only me; that there was no need to get scared. As I realized the awful look in her eyes, I started to look back to see what she was seeing in dreadful horror.

As I turned around, I saw a pack of wolves a few feet behind me, growling with their mouth wide open, showing sharp, ghastly teeth, and dripping drool from the corners of their mouth. They were hungry, very hungry and they were going to rip my flesh apart with their bare teeth and feed on my insides. I scurried back a few steps as they advanced towards me. I looked around for something to defend myself, but saw nothing but wilted grass. One of the wolves lunged at me with a swift jump and before I could feel his paws digging into my skin, I realized he had gone right through me, as if I were.....non-existent. I saw him as I turned around and he was baring his teeth again in front of Shreya who was now frozen with fear. I tried to grab the hair at the back of his neck, but my hand went through him and I knew I had no control over the events that were to unfold in this nightmare; I was just an apparition. Soon after, the wolf lunged again and went for Shreya's neck, digging his canines into her and sprouting a fountain of blood from her jugular. She was looking at me now with a blank expression, as if to ask 'How could you let this happen Arjun? I thought you would always be there for me...that you would protect me...always. I hope I can forgive you for this someday my love...I only wish I can someday'. The others joined him as they dug into the flesh of her arms and thighs as I stood there watching in absolute horror. I looked around and all the pretty lavenders had turned black and were now oozing out a red revolting liquid, and I could taste it where I stood, pathetic and helpless. It was blood, dank and putrid.

I saw the tree where Shreya had been standing and now just saw the wolves, eating pieces of red tender meat, like a family. I saw their snouts covered with her blood and their paws scratching and tenderizing the human meat.

I walked up to the tree and saw the toy train lying on its side. I picked it up and saw that it was smeared red all over with little chunks of warm flesh. I realized I was screaming and screaming some more, as the toy train looked at me helplessly. And the turning wheels of the wooden train were screaming with me.....

One of the little wolves left his meat and walked over to me. My feet were now dug deep into the moist mud with the blades of grass teasing my thighs. He sniffed at me with his red nose and opened its mouth as if to tell me that this was all my creation, I had wanted all this, and they were just my minions doing their job.

'Arjun....Arjun...' he said instead.

I looked into the yellow eyes of the little beast and begged him to devour me and finish the job; that I didn't have a reason to live anymore. But he now stood on his hind legs reaching his paws up to my shoulders and started tapping them hard as I heard a squeal from the black flowers surrounding me. They were screaming at me. They were screaming over and over again.

'Wake up Arjun...you have to wake up now...she's going into...'

The voice trailed off into darkness and I found myself suddenly face first into a staring contest with the fluorescent tray of blue lights on the ceiling. I saw Amit with his hand on my shoulder and knew that *it wasn't a dream, it was never a dream.*

Before opening my eyes from that torrid dream, I knew Shreya was gone. Gone forever.

(7)

24ᵗʰ October 2010

The Eloquent Drunkard.

It was a day before Diwali and I was sitting outside the radiologist's office waiting for my reports. I had not been keeping well since the last three or four months and had begun to look emaciated. Where my cheeks had once been, it had begun to look like hollow caves and my eyes personified empty carved out sockets. As if Shreya's death had not wrecked everything in my life, *it was that damned letter that had put the final nail in the coffin. It had broken me beyond repair.* I waited for the radiologist to come out and tell me what I knew already. He called me to his room and offered me a chair opposite himself.

'Dr. Arjun, we have found something in your X-Ray and it is quite possible that you have been infected since some time now.' He said adjusting his spectacles over his crooked nose.

I stared at him blankly and waited to tell me what I had expected all along.

105

'Here, have a look at your X-Ray'. He said and handed me the black film of dismay.

I looked at the film and it agreed with the diagnosis I had already made and accepted. I nodded and handed it back.

'Tuberculosis.' I said as he looked at the small grape shaped whitish opacity in the middle of my right lung.

He nodded with his index finger rubbing his chin and looked non-chalant. He asked if I wanted another X-Ray done to confirm but I denied the offer. I had known this almost for a month now. He offered me the number of the Physician who worked at the T.B Centre of the hospital and I folded the paper and put it in my pocket.

'Be sure to start treatment as soon as possible.' he said as I took the X-Rays, thanked him for his time and left the room.

I took the elevator (which was functional this time around) and pressed the button for the seventh floor. As the corroded and antique lift made its stops through the floors, I found myself utterly numb and uninterested in the daily proceedings. I did not care or think for a second what I had just been told. *Melancholy – they say is what this is.* As the doors opened, I coughed a little and got out among the crowd of patients, the coughing sounds of some of whom clouded mine. Reaching the ward, I saw Vibhor running towards me in anticipation.

'So, what is it?' he asked.

'You know what it is.'

'Oh man, I'm sorry. I have been telling you for so long to eat properly and come to work. Look at yourself man. You look like one of those lingerie models from Paris, when they start dieting. You know this hospital is a deathtrap, don't you.' He said to my bored face.

'I know, I know and I've been trying my best.' I said hoping that would conclude this unwelcome lecture.

'If this is your best, I don't even want to see your worst buddy. I just hope it isn't drug resistant or something.'

'Thanks for your kind words, Vibhor. If you don't mind and even if you do, I have patients to see now, okay.' I said ending with a deep puffed sigh.

'Okay, okay grouchy pants; I was just worried a little.'

'What, you a chick now?' I said as I punched his arm and we shared a small laugh.

The room of the patients admitted under me was almost empty now. Most of them had gone home for Diwali, I guessed. Only two beds were occupied in the dimly lit room. One was a fresh admission whom I had unfortunately revived the previous day out of a cardiac arrest, bringing him back to this wretched world and other was the alcoholic, Kishori Lal. The near death experience holder was asleep but Kishori Lal was wide-awake and looking out the window. He had gotten both better and worse ever since he had been admitted here five months ago. It had become quite a mystery why he would suddenly become sicker after managing to get better every once in a while. After some initial hesitation, I had bonded quite well with him and I had hated myself whenever I remembered our first meeting. Nevertheless, he had become my sole purpose of not being driven towards insanity, and I had made my mind to improve his case scenario. This was more for me than for him. *I had needed a reason to live, to get out of bed every morning.* This was, thankfully, one of his better days.

'Where's Bhola?' I asked as he greeted me with his hands joined together in unison.

'He has gone out to get something to eat, *Doctor sahib*. I sent him as I didn't want him to torture himself with the hospital food.' He said as I approved with a grin.

'So, how are you feeling today?' I asked as I ruffled through his recent reports.

'Can't complain, *Doctor sahib*. When you are here, I'm never worried.' He said with what felt like genuine gratitude.

'Here, have some please.' He said as he offered me an open box of orange *laddoos*.

'Kishori Lal, I've told you a million times not to eat anything from outside, why do you do this? All my efforts are wasted every time.' I said, surprised at myself for feeling a little anger towards him.

'No, *Doctor sahib,* these are for you. I told Bhola to get them this morning from a local sweets shop. I didn't even touch a piece.'

'Oh.' I said feeling a tiny drop of embarrassment and hate towards myself. 'But for what? I mean, what's the occasion?' I said taking one *laddoo* out of the box and putting it in my mouth. *Even my taste buds felt annihilated as the sweet went wasted on me.*

'My youngest son turns twenty four today, *Doctor sahib.*' He said with elation.

'Congratulations Kishori Lal. You must be very proud of him.' I said going back to looking at the reports.

'I am, *Doctor sahib.* Very proud.'

I did the usual physical examination and checked the reports once again.

'Your liver's showing an abscess Kishori Lal; we'll have to drain it tomorrow evening.'

'Whatever you think is right, *Doctor sahib.*'

As I was about to stand up and leave the room, he put his hand on my left shoulder. 'Is something wrong?' I asked.

'*Doctor sahib,* can you sit with me for a few moments, please?' he asked a little cautiously, not to tempt my anger again.

'I have to see other patients too, Kishori Lal and then I have to…..' I had no idea what I was going to do next. I suddenly found my life empty, too empty without any patients to keep me busy. He looked at me, his eyes almost pleading me to sit down and spend some time with an old man. I obliged him and myself, and sat down again. I noticed a cool drizzle had started outside, the small droplets of rain looking like shining pearls against the transparent silvery windows.

'Did you know Doctor *sahib;* I used to be a college professor in Bihar.'

'I wouldn't have imagined that.' I replied.

'I can see that by the way you looked at me the first time I had come here.' He said as I felt a little ashamed remembering the incident.

'It wasn't your fault Doctor *sahib*, even I was ashamed of myself at that stage in my life. I wasn't myself, you see.' He looked down as I nodded in courteous acknowledgement.

'I once had a life Doctor *sahib*, a good one at that. I used to teach English literature at a small college in Kishanganj district in North-eastern Bihar. I had a wife and three sons, two of whom lived separately from us with their own families. All of this, just ten years ago.'

'What happened then?'

'What always happens Doctor *sahib*. Life, life happened. It's never complete without its share of cruel twists and turns. After I retired from the college, my elder sons took over the house and pushed me, my wife Sunita and my youngest son, Shlok out to the streets. We had nowhere to go as Sunita was an orphan and I had inherited that small house from my father who was long gone'. He said wiping a single tear from his eye.

'Bhola lived with his wife and son about four houses away from us and took us in without a second thought; he said he had owed me a debt as I had got his boy admitted in the arts and literature college free of cost and had supervised the boy's performance under my own guidance. But, Bhola was a small time laborer and didn't even have the resources to feed his own family properly. I had then told my son to leave studies for a while and take up some menial job to support the income of the household. He was very good at math, my youngest son and he got a job under an accountant who had his own shop at the local market.' He said and paused for a bit.

I offered him water and waited patiently.

He drank some water and continued. 'One day Doctor *sahib*, my son had to close the shop at night as he had been doing some work balancing sheets of some accounts of the local farmers and other workers in the field. The accountant had gone home much before him and had told him to finish up and lock the shop before going home. He did finish his work that night, but we never saw him again Doctor *sahib*. We waited and waited for him all night, but he never came home.'

'What happened to him?' I asked in mild surprise.

'What the police told us the next morning was that they had found a body in the bushes behind the local water tank, and they asked us to come to the station and identify it. We went to the station and saw our son lying on the cold steel stretcher with closed eyes and a morbid expression over his pale face.

We later found out that while he was on his way back to the house, a couple of local goons tried to rob him. He tried to fend them off telling them repeatedly, that the money wasn't his but they wouldn't listen. After some struggle between them, one of the goons stabbed him in the stomach while the other one held his arms from behind. And he lay there, bleeding and counting his last breaths as we waited for our son to come home and have a meal with us'. He stopped and started looking outside the foggy window. 'He was only seventeen, Doctor *sahib*.'

I put my hand on his and patted it gently. I had no clue of the pain this man had carried on for so long. I looked at him and tried to peel off the layers of hurt and twinge life had covered him with. *Life spares no one, I thought.*

'After my son was gone, a few years later, Sunita left me too. She had never been the same after

Shlok's death, and one day, sitting in a chair by the window, her heart just gave away. That was the first time in decades that I had felt real sorrow in my life. Without her, I felt as if nothing would ever take her place and fill the deep void in my life. *Sadly* for me Doctor *sahib*, the thing I could best replace her memories with was what landed me here, and in your life.' He said and gave me a smile that I couldn't quite understand. *Why would remembering so much sorrow bring a smile to his face at this time?*

'That's when you started drinking.' I said feeling like a cheap detective from an even cheaper mystery novel.

'That's right Doctor *sahib*. I started drinking to forget her, to forget I ever had a son, to forget I was ever a man whose life was more than just misery, not a great one but good just the same. I used to burn through my pension money every month and started getting worse than before. One night, Bhola saw me sitting in the chair on which Sunita used to sit for hours and he noticed I was frothing blood from the mouth. He took me to the local clinic immediately; bless that kind soul, where they told him to take me to Delhi, that they could not help my further deteriorating condition. And here I am, almost half a year down the line, a little better in my life and eyes because of you, Doctor *sahib*.' He said with a smile.

I greeted his regards with a polite smile.

'It's nothing to be thankful for Kishori Lal; I'm just doing my job.'

'I'm not thankful to you for doing your job Doctor *sahib*. I'm thankful to you, with all my heart, for *caring*. That certainly wasn't your job, and still you did it anyway. That is what marks the character of a man's soul Doctor *sahib*, how he treats the ones beneath him.'

'You don't know me well enough to say all these things Kishori Lal.' I said looking away towards the rain speckled glass window.

'I know enough Doctor *sahib*, and I certainly beat you in experience, don't I?' he raised his eyebrows and I smiled for a few seconds.

'Now, you owe me a debt Doctor *sahib*.' He said with a serious face.

'Debt? What kind of debt?' I asked, puzzled at the man's request.

'The debt of your story, what else. I have shared my past and my sorrows with you, now it's your turn Doctor *sahib*. I know you have been carrying your sorrows over your shoulders ever since I've been here, and you never would have told me if I hadn't compelled you to do so somehow.'

'What are you talking about? I am not upset over anything; I have a very good life.' I tried to weasel my way out of the situation.

'Agreed Doctor *sahib*, but then why are you taking the time out to be with a dying old man, when you could be anywhere, doing any other thing right now?' he had caught me, *experience did count for a lot.*

I had no answer for him and shook my head. 'How did you know?' I asked him.

'You remember that first day when I was admitted here and all that food got spilled over you?' he asked as I nodded and smiled.

'What you had said then, all those words you never had meant to say but still they came out, bursting like a teased dormant volcano, that was not anger at me or anybody else Doctor *sahib*. That was the *pain* you had tried so hard for some time to push deep

117

inside you so that no one, not even your closest, could see it or ask about it. And in that one moment of misfortune, it had reared its ugly head and come hustling out for air and attention.' He said as I looked at the raindrops sliding and merging into one another across the window.

'Now, are you going to tell me your sorrow and pay back your debt, Doctor *sahib*?' he said as he kept his hand on my arm and I admired his honest genuineness.

I got up on my weak legs and told him to get some rest, and that we would talk later. As I turned around to walk away before I felt any more pathetic and vulnerable than I already did, he was still looking at me.

'Doctor *sahib*, what if I die tomorrow? Won't you owe me something for all your life?' He asked in a way that demanded a reply.

I stood in mid-stance, stopped in my steps by a strange request from this man of a small district in Bihar, and I thought. *Really* thought about it. *Could I afford to be indebted to this man for life? Was my life so cheerful already that I could carry this over my head too?*

As I stopped and turned around to sit down, the man from Kishanganj smiled like a small child.

I told him everything, about Shreya, her death and the misery and guilt I had felt after she had left me. Told him everything, *except the letter. That,* I had decided to take to my grave. He listened, listened to every word, patiently, thoughtfully as if he had wanted to hear these things for a long time.

After I had finished, I felt a lump, the size of a golf ball in my throat, and drank some water to drown it, and drown the tears that were to come soon. He looked at me with a kind look in his eyes, the one look you don't really see much nowadays, not even from your closest. I did not match his gaze for a while and kept fidgeting with the stethoscope in my hands that had started shaking a little now. He put his warm, wrinkled hand on them and I somehow gathered the courage to look him in the eye. *Look a patient in the eye with whom I had shared the deepest sorrow of my life.*

'When was the last time you cried, Doctor *sahib?*' he asked.

'I don't really remember, why do you ask?' I tried to avoid answering the question and my fingers grasped the bottle of water again.

'Why don't you answer?' countered the tricky old man.

'I guess I don't really remember, to be honest. It's been quite some time now.' It wasn't completely honest of me though. After what had seemed like a few decades, I had cried my eyes out when I had read Shreya's letter a few weeks back and it had broken me in ways I couldn't have ever thought possible. *It had broken something, some intangible thing, deep down and lurking behind some closed doors in my essence.* I had surprised myself by being able to get up every morning and come to work, probably because somewhere deep in its core, my mind knew it was the only thing that could keep me from crossing the thin line between the brightness of this world and the dark depths of total insanity. *It was the only way to go on, and it was the only thing that made sense any more, even if just a little.*

'Why haven't you cried till now Doctor *sahib*? The sorrow you have endured is by no means a small one, and quite enough to break even the toughest of men.' He said but I could see it in his eyes he knew I had lied.

'I don't know how to explain it to you, Kishori Lal.' I felt cornered now.

'Try me; I'm not that illiterate as you think I might be.' He said and smiled politely.

'I don't think of you like that, and you know it. You've been one of the best patients I've had in a long time. It's just that, *maybe* I'm still in denial about it. Denial is one of the stages of...'

'The five stages of loss, Doctor *sahib*? I might be a little aware of that.' He interrupted and I felt like I had insulted the man once again, but nevertheless impressed at the same time.

'Yes, that is correct.'

'Are you waiting for something, Doctor *sahib*? To change or happen?'

'I'm not sure I understand your question.'

'I just asked, because it's too late now to still be in denial and you don't seem to be the sort of a man who gets angry and bargains with a higher power to set your life right. So if I'm not mistaken Doctor *sahib*, the only thing that makes the case is…' he stopped to look at me thoughtfully and to carefully evaluate my reaction.

'Depression? You think I might be in depression? I can assure you Kishori Lal, that is certainly not the case. Depressed people don't get out of bed in the morning, don't seem to mind their failures in life very much and would certainly not be roaming around in a hospital, of all places. So no, depression is a luxury I can't afford, my friend.' I had lied again.

I had been seeing a private psychiatrist for about three months now, and had been on anti-depressants for two of them. She had asked me if I felt depressed all day long and I had said, that the depression was getting too depressed being with me all time, so it had left me too. She had chuckled about it, like a good psychiatrist humoring her zany patients. The pills had made things much worse than before though, they were making me endure the frequent mood changes that I had hated so much to see in other people. *Crazy man has to take the pills though, that is what it is.*

'Then what are you waiting for, if you are *not* depressed?'

He had caught me somehow and wasn't about to let me go that easily this time around. I shifted in my seat a little and even before I could speak, a tangy sensation rose from my stomach spreading through my throat, and into my mouth. I sighed in a pang of sadness.

'Anger and sorrow are not two different things Doctor *sahib*, as most of us suppose them to be. Both are like a hot flaming piece of coal one holds in his hands, one day hoping to throw it away at someone, and one does too. But only after it has burned deep enough and caused irreparable damage to oneself. He doesn't throw it away immediately because it feels familiar to him, it feels like *his own*. He feels attached to it somehow, as if it is the only thing can fill the empty void of his existence. You on the other hand, Doctor *sahib*, don't belong to that category of people.' He said as I saw a bird feed its younglings by the window seal.

'I don't understand.' I said, my vocal cords suddenly not responding to my wish to speak in audible voice.

'You, Doctor *sahib* belong to the minority of people unfortunate enough to be in it. Somehow, you have trained your mind to become numb to the pain, *to not acknowledge and feel it through your senses.* And for what you don't feel, you don't think to do anything about it. That hot lump of coal will burn through your hand, and the fire will spread viciously to the other parts of your body and mind. Because you won't allow your mind to acknowledge that you are burning, your mind will not tell you to get rid of it.'

'It is like a bottomless pit of despair, you keep falling, hoping one day you'll hit the ground and wake up, but the ground never comes, and you'll keep falling. *And the pain and heat from that flaming coal will never be close enough to finally pierce your senses and tell you to throw it away.'* He said, calm as ever.

I heard everything and realized every word of what he had said. But that black piece of coal was all that I had left of her, *it was the only memory I had now.*

'I owe her this.' I said weakly.

'What do you feel you owe her, Doctor *sahib*?'

'I owe her my suffering, my pain and all that is fair to her. If I was the one who was meant to save her

124

and didn't, it will only be me who has to pay her back somehow. This is her *debt* on my soul, and I'll pay it for the rest of my days till I get to see her again, from far away in hell where I deserve to be in this life and after.' I said as I sniffed and rubbed my eyes.

'You think you can pay her debt with your sufferings, Doctor *sahib*?'

'I think it's the only way I can face her now. The only way I can bear to see myself in the mirror every day. *There is no other way.*' I said as I wiped a single tear, which was too stubborn to settle inside.

'You really loved her with all your heart, did you not?'

'I did, and I still do. But I never deserved to. That's what's killing me the most.'

'If you have truly loved anybody in your life Doctor *sahib*, then you know some debts can never be repaid. No matter how hard you try, how much you're willing to suffer for it, how much you try to lie and tell yourself you've done enough, they'll still be there, *no enough will ever be enough.*'

I kept silent and looked towards the rain-drenched trees outside, the leaves dancing with fervor at the sudden joy of a downpour.

'Do you want to know why that is, Doctor *sahib*?' he asked as I looked at him blankly.

'Because love Doctor *sahib*, unlike other things in this world, is *not* a debt. It is the one pure and untainted thing in the world that doesn't exist if you want it to, and sometimes stays with you, even if you don't want it to anymore. It cannot be created by your own effort; it is something whose origins cannot be defined. It would be as if telling yourself that you can see the wind or feel the light of the sun. It is something that is intangible, effortless and effervescent at the same time.'

'It is the biggest gamble we make in our lives sometimes, and it can reward us back brilliantly or scorch the soul in unimaginable ways as well. It is the one thing we cannot give, cannot take, cannot explain or comprehend. But when you do start seeing the wind and feeling the sunlight, you know it's love and nothing else. *It is a feeling and that quite simply, is what it is.*' He continued as I listened patiently.

'Something else that exists too is what you would call Destiny. It was my son's destiny to get late that day and cross paths with his destiny, and it was my destiny to grow old with his memories, not with him. Sometimes, we decide to choose our own and sometimes, it decides to choose itself for us.'

'So maybe it is my destiny to suffer for what I've done then, is it not?' I said, now feeling the moist touch of tears against my cheeks.

He kept his hand on my shoulder and patted it gently. 'Doctor *sahib*, you are too young to reach that conclusion. As you will grow old and age with time, you'll come to realize a very simple yet conniving fact of life – *You can choose only your own path, not of anyone else*. It was your fiancé's choice to do what she considered right, not yours. Moreover, she made that choice, she chose her path for reasons you cannot subject yourself to be a part of. Now, you have to choose your own.'

'You can choose to be like the river, which has to keep flowing gracefully, or you can stick to the first rock you find and decide to spend your life hiding behind it. *But, remember that a river doesn't choose to flow, it has to flow. Just like life has to go on.* We just have to try and make do with what little we have Doctor *sahib* and never forget that in life, *there are no coincidences.'*

'But is it not unfair, what had I done to anybody to have deserved this? And why her, why the one person who I had closest to my heart?' I felt a hint of anger bubbling up.

'It is very true Doctor *sahib*. Life is not fair to most people. It is not fair to you, the same way it is not fair to Bhola and his family and to thousand others who sleep empty stomach on the roads in cold nights. It is not life which is at fault most of the times Doctor *sahib*, it is we who are so entangled in our affairs of everyday routine, that we expect everything to go our way without any real effort.'

'We have the privilege of seeing some moments of so much joy that we cannot learn to welcome sorrows into our lives, although knowing deep down that both are two sides of the same coin. A man who has never experienced happiness in his life is quite truly, the most blessed man alive Doctor *sahib*, simply because of the fact that the one who does not know joy, will not acknowledge any sorrow. All his sorrows will be his way of life, the only life he has learnt to live by.'

'I understand what you're trying to say.'

'So, now tell me now Doctor *sahib*, why have you not cried till now?' he asked with a sense of accomplishment.

'I...I feel sad.' I stuttered. 'I remember her every day and I feel the sorrow creeping up inside me, jolting me to cry, but I don't. I feel if I cry and let it out, I won't be able to get it back again. Get back the sorrow I feel remembering her, reminding me of the times we were together, *bridging* me to her somehow, in thought. I don't want to lose what little I have left of her now.'

'I am not telling you to forget her Doctor *sahib*, and neither am I saying it would be easy or will get easier soon. Grief takes its own time to work; it feels like a poisonous snake roaming inside us, ready to sting at any moment, but it's a poison that cleanses us from the inside out. But we have to let it work, you see.' He said as I admired the man silently who had given me an antagonistic first impression.

'One thing I can assure you of Doctor *sahib*, is that nothing is stationary in this life, joy or sadness, they both are just guests of a few fleeting moments. It is wise to acknowledge them as so.'

'What about the pain I feel every day? Will it ever go away, if I really want it to?' I asked like a small child lost in the dark woods of a forest.

'You cannot make it go away Doctor *sahib*, it does not work that way. The best you can do is to make your peace with it, identify it as a passing guest in your life and let it stay for as long as it wants to. One day, you will realize that it isn't weighing you down so much as it used to before. And you'll have to keep the faith alive that someday, the sadness will evaporate on its own and you'll be able to sense and feel the little joys of life again.'

'I do hope one day I can recollect your words and act on them.' I said as I kept my hands on his and smiled.

'I hope so too, Doctor *sahib*. I really do.' He said returning the smile.

'Thank you for trying to help me, I do feel a little better now.'

'Don't bury me with your gratitude Doctor *sahib*, I just wanted to share whatever little I have learnt in my life, so that you don't make the mistakes I was too foolish to commit. I just hope maybe someday, I could be of use to you, Doctor *sahib*.'

'I think you've done more than enough, Kishori Lal.'

'You know something, Doctor *sahib*...' he hesitated.

'Tell me, what is it?' I said calmly.

'My son would have been about your age now Doctor *sahib*, if he was still with us. And being around you for the last so many months, I felt as if he was still with me for some time again.' He said with watery eyes, as I felt teary again but composed myself this time.

'I'm sure he's in a much better place now.' I rustled up some words, not exactly knowing how to comfort a man who had just tried his best to show me a tiny speck of light in the darkness.

'I know he is, Doctor *sahib*. I know he is.'

'Umm...I forgot to tell you something, Kishori Lal. I won't be here for a while, as I have to go to the TB clinic on rotation for a couple of weeks. But I will tell Dr. Vibhor to take good care of you; don't hesitate to bother him in any way you want, okay.'

'It is all right, Doctor *sahib*. You have to do what you have to do. Do not worry much about me, I will be just fine. The senior doctors told Bhola today that if my reports came normal for a couple of days, they could think of letting me go home soon.'

'That's great news Kishori Lal. Finally, you could go home and eat some real food, eh?' I chuckled and he joined me.

'Just don't leave without saying goodbye, okay? I'll be glad if you come and see me before you go home.'

'Do not worry, Doctor *sahib*. No doubt, we will meet again. I owe you a lot.'

I patted his shoulder and said goodbye. As I was about to leave the room, he called me from behind.

'See you soon, Doctor *sahib*.' He said with a kind smile I could not fully comprehend but all the same I waved to him and left the ward.

(8)

7th September 2010
Shreya's Letter.

It was an unusually hot September afternoon the day I had decided to go to Shreya's house and meet Mr.Kapoor. He had called me a few days back and had told me he wanted to see me soon. I had told him I would take time out soon to visit, though I had been quite unoccupied at the time. I was not keeping well those days; the coughing had reached troubling proportions and I had lost a good amount of weight. But that wasn't the reason I had wanted to put off visiting my once to be in-laws. It was that house, that damn duplex and everything about it, that reminded me of Shreya every time I passed it on the way. I had called maasi a few times and she had told me to come over, that she'd wanted to see me. I held her off most of the times, promising to make it sometime soon.

I had not met her after the last time I had seen her, when I had stood silently holding her trembling hand, while Mr.Kapoor had lit the sandalwood in flames under Shreya's lifeless body. I had felt alone and miserable, and had missed her a lot the first few

133 ·

weeks. But I knew if I had met her and broken down in front of her, it wouldn't have been of much help to her grieving soul. I had decided that if I couldn't comfort her, I wouldn't burden her with my sadness. It was damn selfish of me and I had felt ashamed leaving her alone at such a time, *but I knew no other way.*

I parked in front of their house and stood outside for a few seconds. The house had now seemed like a dreaded monster that had ingested in its fiery cauldron of a belly, all the best hopes and memories of my life. *I have no purpose being here, I thought, and decided to turn around and leave that forsaken place, never to come back again.* As I turned my back to the house, I thought of maasi and how she had been the mother I never had, how she had made me believe I could do something in life when there was no one else to do so. I had owed her enormously.

Just thinking about it made me feel more like a piece of shit for not being there in her time of need. *You will have to do this, you spineless freak. You can't run this time around.*

I turned back and took small steps towards the house, all the while trying to hold my breath so that I don't even remotely get a scent of lavenders and vomit all over the place. But I couldn't hold my breath, and there was no scent. That made me sad for reasons I couldn't understand. *It made me nauseous every time, but it was a memory of her nevertheless, I thought.* I knocked on the door as the doorbell did not attempt to make any sound, and Mr.Kapoor opened the door after a couple of knocks. I greeted him with a formal *Namaste* and went inside after him. I sat down on the couch opposite him and the television set. He offered me some water but I declined politely and asked him why he had wanted to see me all of a sudden.

'It's about her.' He said and waved his eyebrows towards the kitchen. 'She's not well, Arjun. Doesn't even talk much these days. I have tried to comfort her in every way possible, but she just doesn't seem to be herself.'

I listened quietly with my hands on my knees and fingers intercrossed, feeling like a useless and pathetic waste of life. I saw that he had stern pity in his eyes before he spoke again.

'Arjun, I don't understand something. When Shreya was still with us, you used to come over all the time with one thing or the other. And you knew I did not like it one bit, but couldn't say anything because *my wife* loved you too much, loved you like a son.' He said pointing to the kitchen again.

'She did so much for you Arjun, and this is how you choose to repay her?' he asked with the slight exasperation of a man who feels utter disappointment in someone he trusts just a little too much.

I had my head down in shame and listened like a child, being scolded for something he should have done right. *But it stings more, if you hear it as a grown man.* 'Uncle, I…' I started.

'You what? Didn't have the time for her after her only daughter, *and your fiancé* died?' He interrupted with force.

'It's not that, uncle. I was just having a tough time on my own and didn't want to add to her problems.' I said starting my sorry excuses again.

'You know something Arjun, it was always clear that I did not like you much and maybe the feeling was mutual, I don't know and don't care much about it. I always felt you were a needy child, and she didn't make it better by smothering you so much with her affections.' He said as I looked up at him.

'However, I had and *still have* a lot of respect for your father. He is an admirable man in the best sense of the word. No matter what he faced and how much struggle I have seen him go through, he never once complained or made any excuses about any damn thing. In fact, and you should probably know this now, it was only because of him, that I had agreed for you and Shreya to be together. It pains me to say this Arjun, but you're not even half the man your father is, and never will be if you keep at your ways. A man like your father would never turn his back on his own if life got a little prickly under the feet.' He said sternly as I felt too numb to react to the insults, partly because I knew what he said to be true, that I was not like my father, that *I was not a worthy man.*

'I did not call you here today to insult or belittle you, Arjun. I know you must be going through a lot right now, and I know you loved Shreya a lot; but I have to know what you're thinking, what you think you want to do now. It is never easy to lose someone close to us, but at the same time, we have to think of those who still depend on us. We can run only a certain distance before life catches up, you know. One day, you have to take stock of it.'

'I know uncle. I know what I have to do.' I said as I stood up and made my way to the kitchen. *I had deserved every bit of it, I told myself. At least it felt a little better now.*

I walked in to the kitchen and saw maasi standing behind the stove. I walked up to her, jitteriness in my steps, and kept my hand on her shoulder. She turned around, and for a fleeting moment, I thought she hadn't recognized me at all. She just stood there and looked at me with waiting eyes. After a few dry and agonizing seconds, she put her hand on my bony cheek and gave me a painful smile.

'Arjun, you *finally* came, I'm so happy to see you *beta.*' She said as she felt the bony ridges on my cheek and winced.

'My god Arjun, what have you done to yourself? You look *sick*, my son. You are not eating well these days, are you?' she asked with such an honest motherly concern that my insides hurt with remorse. I had wanted her to slap me hard across my face, not once, not twice, but as much as she wanted to. But she didn't do anything to hurt me, didn't even scold me or shout at me for what I had done to her. *She wasn't going to make this easy; I thought to myself and cringed.* I forced a smile and touched her feet. I should've kissed them instead, for what she had done and been to me for the past two decades of my life.

I took the pot off the stove and poured her some tea. Uncle had gone out for his evening walk and we sat down in the living room. I had never been in their living room much as Mr. Kapoor used to be sitting there all the time, and I had not wanted any piece of that action, ever. But sometimes when he used to be at the bank, most probably screaming over my diligent father, maasi used to make some fried potato wedges for me and Shreya, and the three of us would sit there for hours at end; me and Shreya trying to out-do each other verbally and maasi just sitting and laughing with us. *But it had been a long, very long time since that age. By now, Shreya was nothing but a memory like all the ones I had cherished with her.*

'How are you, maasi?' I asked holding the hot cup of tea.

'Don't worry about me, Arjun. *Teri maasi itni kamzor nahi hai (Your maasi is not so fragile)'.* She said with a weak smile.

'I know, but uncle said that you're not keeping well nowadays.' I said and immediately cursed myself for saying that. *What if she thinks you just came because he had asked you to come?*

'He just worries too much about me. You know Arjun, beneath that grumpy exterior is a very sweet man.' She said and I gave a wry smile. She looked around in the living room for a while and sighed as I slurped the hot tea slowly.

'Do you remember the time Arjun, when we used to sit here, *all of us*? Those are the evenings I think of sometimes; when I want to remember her and cry, you know. I just imagine the two of you fighting and bickering like kids again.' She said and wiped the corners of her eyes.

'I do remember. I can't forget those days even if I try to.' I said looking down at the floor.

'I want to tell you something, Arjun. Something that probably doesn't even matter now, but I would like to tell you just the same. It has been on my mind for many days now.' She said as I looked at her with attention.

'Do you remember the first time you had told Shreya how you had felt about her? What was it, five years ago?'

I laughed, surprising myself at the ability to do so. 'She told you about that?' I asked, my eyes wide with surprise.

'Yes, she did tell me about it. Girls do not hide anything from their mothers Arjun; it's just that kind of a relationship.'

'I guess that's true.' I said with an embarrassed smile. 'So, what exactly did she tell you about that night?'

'She told me what I had known for many years even before you did. She told me how you proposed to her and how it had made her feel at that time.'

'Confused and awkward?' I asked jokingly.

"If I'm not mistaken, I believe the words she had used were 'Special' and 'Happy'. She *was* really happy too. She even showed me that beautiful watch you had given her that day. In fact, maybe I've...' she stopped and got up and went to find something in the bedroom.

'Here it is!' she caught me by surprise as I heard her scream out from a distance.

'I knew I had kept it here somewhere. She only wore this for very special occasions, you see. The rest of the time, it stayed with my cupboards and me. Here, I'm sure you remember this.' She said as she passed on the watch to me.

It had managed to look pretty good even after all these years. I felt the back of the dial and as my fingers felt the alphabets of her name once again, my heart sank. I had to try my best to control any sort of reaction that might further upset *maasi*, so I stretched my hand to give it back to her.

'You keep it Arjun; it has no one in this house to take care of it now.' She said as I closed my wrist over the little silver timekeeper.

'Why was she happy that night? She did tell you what had happened next, right?'

'She did, and there was a reason for it too.'

'Can I ask what it was?'

'She had told me that you weren't ready back then, that she felt it in your voice somehow. That you had hesitated a little.'

'Of course I had hesitated. It's not like taking a walk in the park when you're about to propose such a beautiful girl, is it?' I said as we both laughed a little.

'Well, whatever it was, she was glad you told her how you had felt about her.'

'I still feel the same way.' I said almost to myself, as my fingers remembered the sensation of her name behind the dial of the watch.

'I haven't even been to her room since she has left us. Just can't find the courage to do so. I just tell the maid to change the sheets every once in a while. You can go and spend some time in there, *if you would like to.'*

I hesitated a little, not knowing what to say to her then. I could have said no to the request and break her heart, break the heart of the woman who had borne so much already and decided not to. 'Sure, I'll go upstairs *maasi.'*

'You don't have to, if you don't want to.'

'No *maasi*, I want to.'

As I stood up to make my way upstairs and face my demons, she said to me 'I still miss her a lot on some days, Arjun.'

I gave her a hug and told her that I felt the same way, that it was going to get better in a while.

I stood outside Shreya's room for a while, not able to decide whether to go in or not. *You could always tell her that you went in, felt good about it or something meaningful that'll put her mind at ease, you could do that. Or you could go inside and see what death feels like, immersed in every air and dust particle that floats in that room. What the hell, it's time to be a man for a change.*

I pushed the door a little, and it opened with a wooden creaky sound.

As I went inside, I realized the air was heavy and stale. *Not a sense of stench, just dense air that refuses to go into the lungs.* I closed the door and looked around the room. It seemed implausible that, this had once been the place where I had once felt an incomparable joy. I went to the far end of the room and opened up the window, hoping the air would get breathable somehow. I sat on the bed for a while, feeling the soft fabric of new sheets against my rough hands. *She had been sitting here when you had proposed her, and it was probably here that she had decided to cut herself too, my inner voice blared out of the blue like an intolerable siren.*

'Shut up, just shut the hell up.' I said to the empty room and pressed my head with my hands. *You thought it would be that easy? That you'd just come here, look around, take a few deep sighs and move on with your life? Don't keep fooling yourself, you pathetic waste of life.*

'What do you want? What the hell do you want me to do then?' I screamed and saw myself in the mirror in front of me on the dresser.

The image in the mirror seemed different now. It was me all the same, with the same clothes, but the expression had changed into an angry version of myself. *'You damn well know what I want!' it said with an anger scorching like fiery red flames in its eyes. 'I want you to remember. I want you to fucking remember, you piece of shit!' it said angrily.*

'I don't know what you're talking about. Go fuck off somewhere and leave me alone! For God sake's please leave me alone!' I pleaded.

'Oh don't worry, I'll leave you alone. Right after I've minced your brain into such fine pulp that you won't know your shithole from your mouth. And you'll like it just the same; you'll like it when I screw your brain to the wall!'

'No, please stop…please; I don't know what to remember. I don't know what…' I begged it to listen to my pleading requests and put my hands on my face again, sobbing like a child. I kept crying and pleading for about ten minutes, which had seemed like an hour. Then, I finally remembered. *Remembered her last words.*

I got up from the bed and opened the cupboard full of clothes, which almost fell all over and buried me. I kept them on the dresser and started looking, *digging* with my hands. Nearly the whole collection in the closet was on the dresser and the bed when I finally saw it. *The toy train.* A childhood memorabilia that had found a way to get caught up in things somehow. *Why couldn't you have kept it for yourself? I thought to myself* while holding it in my hands and spinning its little wheels. I looked down again, and grasped the blue journal between my fingers and pulled it out from the cupboard. *Let's do this, I declared to myself.*

I pushed aside the clothes that I had stacked up on the bed and sat in the middle with the journal in my hand. I opened it and saw an envelope sticking out at the end with the letter A written in big and red. I took it out and threw the journal on one of the teddy bears, which now lay on its face like an injured soldier, at the back of the bed. After tearing it carefully from the top, I took out the letter and unfolded it with jittery hands.

'My dearest Arjun,

When you will find this letter, I would have been long gone and you would probably hate me more than ever. I deserve every bit of your hate, to leave you like this. But I guess, life turns out a little different than we ever imagine it to be. You must've thought about why I did what I did, and I can only imagine the hurt it would have caused you till the time you had found this letter. Therefore, it's only right that i tell you upfront, this was not an impulsive decision. I had struggled with this for many months before finally deciding to end my life. It was getting too painful to live on Arjun, and I owe it to you to explain why I had decided to do this. I do hope you get all your answers from this letter.

It was the day of my graduation and Aashita and I had decided to go clubbing at night to celebrate the occasion. We reached the club around seven and went inside. I had told Aashita earlier not to drink too much and to stay with me all the time we would be in there, as I knew she always got flirty after a few drinks and I had to keep her out of trouble. We danced for a while and after a few songs, I went to the bar for a drink. Aashita was still in her own, it was amazing how she could dance for so long without any alcohol in her. As I was sitting there, watching her on the dance floor, the bartender gave me a drink before I had even ordered anything. I asked him about it and he told me that the guy sitting a few chairs away at the bar table had sent it for me. I gestured my appreciation of the offer, but declined the drink politely. A few minutes later, he came over, introduced himself as Aashita's friend Rajat, and waved to her at the dance floor, and she waved back to him. I talked to him for a while and had a drink with him. He left after a few minutes to dance with Aashita again as I began to feel a little dizzy sitting at the bar counter.

I must've fallen asleep for a short while on the bar counter, when I felt a hand on my shoulder. I woke up but was still very drowsy and I saw that it was Rajat again and he was asking me whether I was all right or not. I told him to go and get Aashita, so that we could leave. He told me Aashita was waiting for me outside and he had told her he was going inside to get me. As I was feeling too drowsy to even stand properly, he helped me up and we made our way *through the crowd to the exit door. As I was going through the door, I hit my head against something hard and fell unconscious.*

What comes next won't be as easy to hear, but I have to tell you everything, so please bear with me my love. When my eyes kept opening and closing in between endless time frames, I vaguely recall seeing the roof of a car from the inside and two men on top, taking their turns with me. I could see that one of them was Rajat and another man, whom I couldn't recognize. I could see them breathing, sweating heavily and talking among themselves, but I just couldn't speak and had lost the ability to move, as I saw that car roof shaking and moving, going up and down and everywhere. It was like waking up into a nightmare. I kept trying to scream and shout, trying to understand what was going on, but they were all shouts in a dream. My face felt drenched with a mixed stench of vomit, tears and sweat as my tongue failed to move out of my mouth. No voice came out from my throat too, as I struggled with gaining consciousness and discerning it from the unreal world. If it gives you some relief, as it had given me after going through this, I would like you to know that, I had felt nothing during that trip to oblivion.'

The words had become a little smudged in this part, and I understood why as I imagined Shreya crying, and her tears making their way down to the paper. I clenched the letter hard between my fingers and felt my own eyes watering up. *I can't read this anymore, I just can't. It's just...just too much to bear. I can't do it, I won't do it.* After composing myself a few minutes later, I read on.

'*When I opened my eyes next, I was lying near the back exit of the same bar with Aashita holding me in her arms and crying my name over and over again. My clothes were not torn but were certainly roughed up a bit, and I felt an excruciatingly painful sting at the back of my head, and between my thighs. I felt down my dress and saw that it was soaked with blood. I tried to ask Aashita what had happened, hoping she'd tell me that I had bumped my head somewhere and fell down the steps, that all of it had been nothing but a bad dream. She told me what had happened, how she had met Rajat or whoever he was, just an hour ago on the dance floor. How she had been dancing casually all the while and didn't notice that a demon had taken me in his arms to where ever he pleased. I realized all of it seemed too true, to be a dream. I realized that, I was raped.*'

I closed my eyes for a while. Everything seemed to stand still around me, the wind had stopped blowing and the chirping birds had become silent. Only the last sentence I had just read, was echoing through my mind like an endless parade of shameful failures of the past, *mocking me, humiliating me.* It seemed too real to happen, to anyone. My chest felt heavy all of a sudden and the throbbing headache had returned with a vengeance. I felt a lot of emotions in that moment – shame, guilt, anger, sorrow, misery. However, the one thing that had overshadowed them all, was pure and utter *helplessness. Helplessness, like she would have felt in those moments.*

The one thing that I realized in all my misery in those few minutes, was the simple truth that no matter how far you go in life, you can never own it. *Life owns all, and screws up whomever it wants to screw. A plain and simple truth. This must be what hell feels like, I thought to myself as tears, for the first time in what felt like decades, rolled down in a flurry.* I didn't realize the time it took for me to gather the courage to start reading again.

I was in no condition to talk or listen to anyone for a few weeks. I had closed myself in my dorm room. Everything had seemed distant, fake. But I tried my best to forget it and get over it with a lot of help from Aashita, who was in tears with me all the time and blamed herself for everything. Somehow, in a month or so, I had forgotten about the incident, easier as it was by my lack of awareness of what had happened. People say if you don't remember it, maybe it didn't happen. Don't know how much of that is true, though. I had called mom and dad and had told them I would be staying for a while longer to finish up some pending projects, so that they don't suspect something and worry about it, and you were too busy as it is.

Some weeks later, I began to feel a little unwell and had bouts of vomiting almost every morning. At first, I thought it was a stomach infection and took some antibiotics for it. When they didn't seem to work at all, Aashita took me to a small private gynecologist in the local area. She did the tests and confirmed my worst fears. I was almost one and a half months pregnant. I had gone in expecting this to some extent and it didn't hit me as hard as I would have imagined. I talked to the Doctor and explained my situation, that how my pregnancy had not been my wish at all. She calmed me down and talked me through it, explaining to me the option of abortion; and Aashita and I agreed to have the procedure as soon as possible.

You remember that evening, when we had that little talk on your front porch, Arjun? I had already undergone the abortion by then, but just wanted to know how you felt about the situation of a single, pregnant woman. Well, you had made your opinions quite clear about it, not that you were wrong, but I got the message just the same.

After everything had happened, I felt I could move on with my life, that everything would be all right from there on. But I was wrong, Arjun. So horribly wrong. Three months ago, I had started having nightmares, some too horrid to even describe. However, one of them haunted me almost every other night.

In this dream, I would find myself in a vast open field, a barren and deserted one. I would keep walking along a narrow clearing between the two large patches of yellow dry grass spread over miles. I would be alone, all alone. At first, it would feel oddly serene, but then, suddenly out of nowhere, lightning would strike all over the empty field and the sky would change its color from the pleasant blue it once was, to a ghastly black. Out of nowhere, trees would start emerging from the ground everywhere. But, not trees with green leaves and brown trunks, not at all. The trees would grow, but instead of the long branches, grotesque little bodies would start appearing out of the trees. Horrid and wrinkled tiny structures, with their hands crossed over their putrid bodies and eyes tightly closed in painful agony.

I would walk over to one of the trees and touch one of these creatures with my fingers, which would recoil back in horror on feeling human flesh. And all of them, who had their eyes closed until now, would be awake suddenly, and would start crying, crying in such a shrill tearing voice that

153

would make me scream too. And I would wake up, screaming.

I had tried my best to live with these nightmares, and I really did for some time. But they wouldn't let me go; they wouldn't stop until they had me. The only way I was ever going to beat them was to never be able to dream again. I always feared that one day, these dreams would somehow manifest into a reality, a reality that would be so horribly terrifying for you, that it would mean the end of the road for us. And I didn't want that, ever. Even if fate had turned out this way, I was going to be in charge of my own misfortune. Remember Arjun, when I had asked you why the sun looked orange just before setting? I got the answer one fine evening as I was sitting by the window alone, just two days before I wrote this letter. It's a personification of life Arjun, in some strange way. The 'everyday' of our lives is so incredibly overstuffed with things – both good and bad, that it sometimes becomes necessary to unload from our souls, the weight of it all. As we burn bright like the sun throughout the day, the end represents the excess and useless fuel in our lives burning in a bright orange cauldron. I don't know how much sense anything makes for you when you are reading this, and I won't want to imagine it as well. You might think some things like, that I gave up too easily or even absurd things such as maybe I wasn't happy being with you or something like that. Please don't think of such things, Arjun. I have realized now that such things have to happen, regardless of what we might think or plan to do in life. There's just no point in crying over something you can't possibly control, is there?

Arjun my love, I had once promised you that I'd never leave your side, come what may. I know your mother left you when you were young, and you might think I am doing the same. The sorrow I feel breaking my promise and leaving you alone is beyond any comparison. I feel it aching, my heart, whenever I think of not seeing you again. You are a good man, Arjun and do not let anyone tell you otherwise. It's the kindness in your eyes that pulled me towards you, not a lot of it out there now, so keep it alive inside you. And please don't burden yourself with this, I know it won't be easy for you, but none of this is in any way, your fault. Promise me that you will take good care of my parents and never let them know about this. You will have to be strong, my love and try to move on with your life. I chose my destiny; you have to choose yours now.

Unfortunately, even the last letter we write to someone has to end with some lines. All I can gather at this point of time to say to you is that...It's time to say goodbye, Arjun. We had a good life together my love, and howsoever short it might have been, it made me happy beyond measure.

Take care of yourself and always remember that you will be in my heart, for all eternity. I love you just so much.

Forever and ever yours,

Shreya.

I sat there for a while, with the letter now crumpled up in my hand. My tear ducts had dried up and my brain had taken a leave of absence. For the first time in my life, I had no plan anymore. I didn't know where my steps would lead me now, but the *horror* in this thought was that I knew there was going to be no destination, no far corner of the world, where I'd be at peace again. *Nowhere, where I would ever be me again.*

I put the wrinkled piece of paper in my shirt pocket and searched the pockets in my trousers for a smoke, but I was all out. My head felt like it had a clear suicidal intent, the way it was throbbing and planning to burst open at any second. I tried to stand up and realized I couldn't. Somehow, holding the edge of the cupboard, I stood up and found out my knees had turned into long thin bands of elastic rubber. As the grayness swam over my senses one more time, my wobbly legs gave up the struggle, and my head hit the blunt edge of the dresser on the way down.

Before concluding my one-way journey to the floor, I had lost my bridge to any sense of reality I might have ever known.

(9)

17th November 2010
The Present and Beyond.

The words of Kishori Lal had settled me a bit, and maybe it was the cocktail of anti-depressants and anti-tubercular drugs, but the depression had subsided somewhat. Now, I could look in the mirror and see *myself* on a few good days. However, the insomnia and guilt had still prevailed, and I still yearned badly for Shreya on some days. I had not been to the Medicine ward for a few weeks now and had hoped Kishori Lal got well and had went back home. I reached the hospital around nine in the morning and saw that the back entrance had been closed for some days. I made my way around the college building up to the second floor, where it bridged through a small connector pavement, to the hospital wards. As I reached the connector, I saw a tall man dressed in white at waving his hands towards me. I looked behind me but there was no one. It felt a little strange seeing no one around at that time, *at the peak hour of the hospital.* As I reached the end of the pavement, I saw it was Kishori Lal and it brought a smile to my face.

'*Namaste,* Doctor *sahib*. How have you been?' he said looking a little different than the time I had seen him last. His face was looking quite radiant for a man who had just got a second lease on life. *Looking a little, happy.*

'I'm good Kishori Lal. Looks like you've turned a tide, my friend.' I said to him as I put a hand on his arm.

'It is all because of you, Doctor *sahib*, it is you who has turned it around for me.'

'So, finally going home? Where's Bhola?' I asked looking around.

'He has gone to finish packing our belongings. I will be meeting him just outside in a while. It is time for me to go.'

'It's quite a co-incidence that I met you just before you were leaving. I'm glad to see you back on your feet Kishori Lal, and hope the best for you in life.' I said putting out my hand for a gentleman's shake.

'This will not do, Doctor *sahib*.' He said as he declined my outstretched hand and gave me an unusually warm embrace, which felt a whole lot better than my stupid choice of parting ways with a dear acquaintance.

'Well, a promise is a promise Doctor *sahib*. I told you we would meet again and we did, and I even have something for you.'

'Please, Kishori Lal, no need for anything. I'm just happy that I got to meet you today and see that you're finally going home healthy.'

'Doctor *sahib*, consider this a small token of appreciation from a poor old man. I would like it very much if you would take it from me.' He said as he fished out a small folded paper from the pocket of his white *kurta* and held it out for me.

'All right.' I said taking the folded sheet from him. 'I guess that makes us even, now.' I winked at him as we both laughed a little. We chatted for a couple of minutes more and he took my leave after some time.

'Thank you again Doctor *sahib*, for everything.' He said as he turned around to go back.

'It was my pleasure, Kishori Lal. By the way, what is this?' I asked him gesturing towards the piece of paper he had just given me.

'Why don't you open it later and see for yourself, Doctor *sahib*?' he said with a sly but innocent smile as he waved goodbye and I saw the wise old man from Kishanganj making his way towards a better life.

As I stood there alone, I had an instant urge to open the folded sheet and feed my curiosity. I was about to do it too, when a familiar voice called my name from behind.

'Ajju, what are you doing there? We're late and Thakur's about to blow his lid, c'mon...what are you waiting there for?' Vibhor shouted and I broke into a stride, putting the folded sheet in the breast pocket of my apron.

As I was taking my rounds in the ward and filling the patient forms, I noticed Vibhor was not as chatty as he was most of the time, and was sitting quietly in the duty room. *Must finally be growing up, I thought.* I was drawing the blood sample from one of my patients when he showed up at the room entrance.

'Hey Arjun, bro can I talk to you about something?' he said from behind me.

'Vibhor, I swear to god if you're setting me up for a filthy joke…'

'No, it's not that.' He said with such a serious face that I had trouble recognizing him for a second.

'Okay sure man, just give me a couple of minutes to finish up here.' I told him as he left the room in a confused daze.

I opened the door of the duty room and saw him sitting alone, on the bed with his hands clasped together.

'What's up?' I asked as he looked at the floor.

'Hey, you won't guess who I just saw this morning. Talk about a good start to the day. It was…'

'I wanted to talk to you about your patient in bed 31 Arjun, Kishori Lal.'

'Yeah, I just saw h…'

'He *died* Arjun; he died just two days after you left.'

'What? No Vibhor, you must be thinking of some other patient. Kishori Lal is fine.'

'Arjun, do you see him in the ward?' he asked me with eyes as big as golf balls.

'Of course not, but that's because he got discharged today. And I saw him this morning, *just this morning. And he had looked fit as a fiddle.'*

'Arjun, I had been on duty that night and had made his Death Certificate myself when he had bled out.'

I felt my nerves tingle with a bizarre sensation and felt absurdity taking over my mind. I sat down as Vibhor explained to me the events that had transpired on the night of 29th of October. He told me how he had stayed until night, as Kishori Lal had told him he wasn't feeling well all of a sudden. He told me that Kishori Lal had wanted to talk to me that evening, but my phone was not reachable. He had just caught a wink of sleep when he had heard the cries of Bhola and had rushed to Kishori Lal's bed.

He had seen him vomiting out blood uncontrollably, bleeding out like an artery deciding to end its life. He told me that he tried everything to stop the blood from draining Kishori Lal's body, but no drug or procedure seemed to do anything. The last words he had said, were ' *Doctor Sahib ko bula dijiye...Arjun sahib ko...'* (*Call doctor sahib, please call doctor Arjun*) as he vomited the final few splashes onto the floor and collapsed. It was as if a dam had burst open, Vibhor told me.

'How is this possible?' I said more to myself than to Vibhor.

'Do you want to see the list of patients who have been discharged in the last few days, Arjun?' he asked calmly.

'No, I don't.' I said and felt a surge of anger rising within me. 'What the hell, Vibhor? That patient was under my care for six months and nothing bad ever happened. I leave him to you for a couple of weeks, and he dies in a couple of days!' I snarled.

'Look Arjun, calm down. I already told you I tried everything from drugs to invasive procedures, but nothing seemed to work. The drugs couldn't even elevate his *goddamn* blood pressure; it just kept falling and falling. Even the Senior Resident on duty had confirmed that I couldn't have done anything else to save him.' He explained himself as I tried to reconnect the fried circuits in my brain.

'Tell yourself whatever you want to believe, Vibhor. Whatever helps you sleep at night.' I was still fuming.

'I'm sorry again, brother. I knew you had bonded well with that patient.' He said, as he stood up to leave and patted my shoulder on the way out.

'Maybe you saw someone that looked like him.' He said as he went out and the door closed behind him. But, the only thought that was floating like a trapped bee in my brain, stinging wherever it touched, was – *Why does everyone I begin to care for, die and leave me more miserable than ever?*

I went home that day, tired and unable to reason out things anymore. The night wind had picked up and I felt a cold breeze grazing through my face, as I got out of the car. It was 11.45 pm when I opened the front door and saw dad lying asleep in front of the television again, his legs hanging on the side of the couch. I put them up on the couch with the rest of him and covered him with a blanket after turning off the idiot box. I went to my room and lay on the bed without even thinking of changing my clothes or even move, for that matter. I felt completely exhausted and yet, there was no sign of sleep. A little too much had happened for sleep to come easily anyway. Hours passed by but all I could think about was a panorama of thoughts racing in my head.

Had I hallucinated the whole thing? The whole meeting with Kishori Lal? Were the drugs pushing me into some kind of weird delirium? I knew I had not been feeling like myself for the past few months, but was this really happening? Who can identify the thin line between the real and the insane world? Maybe sometimes, when you decide to walk that slim tightrope, you only need to slip once, and slip badly. All that awaits on the flip side of that rope down below, is a pit of darkness and oblivion. I couldn't even begin to, and was extremely scared to, think about all the other conversations and events I might have imagined. With all the headaches I'd been having, and that brutal fall I had taken to the head a month before, anything seemed possible to my dizzy brain now. Did that mean…I had made up more than I knew?

I sat up on the bed and thought hard. There had to be something I could think of, some conversation I could prove or hold up something tangible to rid my brain of this torrid feeling of lunacy.

I thought hard for about an hour or so, before it finally struck me. Of course, how could I have been so stupid? There was something, or maybe something I had hoped to find that would settle my nerves. The time was 1.58 am when I jumped off the bed and frantically lunged for my apron. I felt the inside of the breast pocket, pale in anticipation that I would find nothing, that I had finally gone berserk.

But there it was, and as I pulled out the folded sheet of white paper, a mighty wave of relief ran through my mind. *I realized I still had some sanity left in me; that my brain had suffered with me, but had not given up yet.* I opened the note with quivering hands, and read it.

My hands stopped shaking as I found myself lying on the bed a few moments later, with tears freely rolling down my shut eyes. ***There are no co-incidences, Doctor sahib***; I remembered Kishori Lal's words as I surrendered my senses to a much-awaited slumber.

The time was 3.07 am on a chilly November morning as I felt the warm soothing touch of her fingers on my forehead for the last time and the cold embrace of longing that had held me all this while, slowly fading away. The scent of white lavenders blossomed through my senses and washed off the black soreness, which had plagued my heart for a period of time I could not recollect.

The Sun would break the horizon in a few hours and I hoped, in a way only a bruised heart really could, that it would be as orange as it could ever be.

(10)

27th September 2008, Sunday

Then, Now and Forever

After the restaurant fiasco about two years back, I had never hoped things would ever go back to normal again. I had not talked to her for a while after that incident in spite of her texts and calls. Every time I had picked up her call, she would say the same thing over and over again – *'Arjun, let's be friends like before na, why can't you let this go yaar? I like being with you, talking to you...please talk to me sometime...I miss you'* and my response would always be a mixture of anger and tired grunting sounds.

This is the thing we men can never understand about the female sex; they really want to be friends with the guys they don't consider fit for the boyfriend category. What they plan to get from such an alliance is beyond the intellect of even the best of men. In any case, after a few months I had begun talking to her once again (*big surprise!*) as I had missed her like hell.

We began talking about the little things again, about her studies, my future plans and other trivial stuff. I used to get out of the library late at nights to call her up sometimes, and I loved her more every time I heard her divine voice. After some time, she mentioned that she had been seeing someone from her own college and really liked the guy. I was somewhat heartbroken on hearing about this new development, though I could not fathom the reason for it. Maybe I still was keeping some hope that eventually she would come back to me after some time. Life's never like the movies, I suppose. It was a different feeling thinking that she had rejected me, that feeling I could have reasoned with. However, to go and be with someone else was beyond rejection; it was an insult no man could bear to take easily. Even after hearing all I could endure, I still kept in contact with her; for reasons I did not want to think of.

As soon as I could gather the courage, I decided to meet her, since it had been a long time I had seen her by then. I had missed Maasi too, unbearably at that. The only time I went to visit her once or twice was when I was sure Shreya wasn't home. It was the one thing that kept me away from her loving touch; the thought of seeing Shreya and tormenting myself once again. Leaving all my tumultuous thoughts behind, I finally decided on paying her a visit.

The time was 3.30 pm on a clear Sunday afternoon when I reached the place. It had become quite cloudy that day, which was quite unusual for that time of the year. 'Just hope it doesn't rain' I said to myself as I hopped up to the front porch and rang the doorbell cautiously.

'Who is it?' a sweet feminine voice I knew too well responded.

"Arjun…Arjun Vashisht" I said trying to sound playful.

A hush of hurried footsteps bundled towards me and before I knew it, my body was being tightly clasped in a warm embrace by Shreya.

'Itne din ho gaye, kahan tha Idiot' (*It's been so many days, where were you Idiot?)* she blurted out with what seemed like genuine happiness.

"You must be mistaken Miss, I came here to meet Mrs. Kapoor. You certainly don't look like her, so can I please be let go now?" I mocked her teasingly, partly in fun, but mostly because as long as she would have clung on to me, the tougher it would have been not thinking about it later.

171

'*Ya Ya* whatever man, who wants to see you anyways, huh?' she said in a huff, letting me go and backing up a bit.

"Well, you kind of answered that question already when you hugged me just now. So that's something to think about." I knew I was bugging her but I had missed all this and did not want to relent.

'Okay Smarty pants, shut up now and come inside.' She said pulling me with one hand and closing the door behind her with the other.

'Mrs. Kapoor, *Aapka laadla aaya hai, ab sambhaalo janab ko aap hi' (Your beloved son has come, you tend to him now)* she shouted towards the kitchen as my nostrils filled up with heavenly aroma of fried food.

As my eyes wandered around the house which seemed oddly empty, my gaze was met by Shreya.

'He's not at home, so relax. I swear to god, you become a jittery bug around him.' She said rolling her eyes with an exasperated expression.

"You would feel the same way if someone looked at you with murderous eyes all the time." I said elbowing her arm from the side and she chuckled too.

'Arjun, *Aa gaya beta'* (*You came my son*) Maasi said in a loving voice from a distance and came close to pat my cheek. *'Kaisa hai tu…Bhool jaata hai tu apni maasi ko'* (*How are you…You keep forgetting your maasi a lot*) she said as I touched her feet and began the usual routine of blushing that came over me whenever I was shown such affection.

"I'm good Maasi, came over just to meet you, as I was missing you a lot". I said looking from the corner of my eye towards Shreya who stood with her arms crossed now.

'Haan haan bilkul theek hai…aap dono pyaar bhari baatein karo, main chali jaati hoon…waise bhi mujhse thodi kisiko baat karni hai' (*Ya both of you continue your lovely talk, I'll just go…it's not as if someone wants to talk to me!*) Shreya said with dramatic effect.

"Oh come here you…" I said as I grabbed her hand and pulled a little playfully.

'Go to hell, you idiot.' came the reply as she pulled her hand away and both of us laughed.

'Hey Bhagwaan (Oh my God), both of you will never change' Maasi said slamming her palm over her forehead as only Indian women do when annoyed.

'Arjun, I have made *Pakodas* and Tea for you, *beta*. Come and wash your hands, I will bring them from the kitchen.' Maasi said as my taste buds signaled red alert on hearing *pakodas*.

'Maasi, you cook so well, teach her a thing or two also na. *Gadhi ko kuch banana nahi aata abhi tak (This donkey doesn't know how to cook anything till now).*' I said as Shreya turned her glance and showed me her full tongue as a classy retort.

We sat for an hour or so, like the good old days. Talking about useless things, me and Maasi teaming up on Shreya and her getting irritated over the unfair disadvantage. I finished my second cup of tea and looked at Shreya. She was fiddling with her left ear-ring and humming an old tune. Only after seeing and talking to her did I realize how badly I had missed her, *how miserable I had been without her.* Maasi caught me staring at Shreya and pinched my arm teasingly.

'Shreya, why don't the both of you go out today? The weather's nice, it will be a good outing for you, no?' she said as I felt even luckier to have her in my life.

'Yeah I think I can go out, what do you think *Buddhu (idiot)* ?' she asked me, breaking up from her thoughts.

"Okay I guess. Maasi, will you be okay alone at home?" I asked.

'You kids go and have fun, I will be alright. Your Uncle will be coming home anytime now.'

'It's decided then...give me five minutes *buddhu* and I'll be right out.' Shreya said halfway up the stairs.

I went and waited for her outside. A stream of random thoughts started to blare their horns in my mind once I realized what I had planned to do. *Maybe this is how it's supposed to end. Maybe it's not meant to be as blissful as you have imagined all along. Maybe all stories don't have a happy ending.*

I was standing outside, leaning against my car and completely lost in my stream of thought, when I felt a punch on my arm.

'Are you waiting for someone else, Dr.Arjun?' she asked winking at me playfully.

I wish Shreya, I really do. I wish I was waiting for someone who knew, I was waiting for her.

The time was 5.10 pm and we were on our way soon enough. The rush hour traffic was already suffocating the life out of the clustered car engines. We were stuck at a red light hardly ten minutes out of the house as I switched on the radio.

"Seen any new movies lately?" I asked as I tuned the radio, which gave out buzzed signals.

'Not really, don't go out much these days. *Waise Bhi(Anyways)*, no movies worth watching nowadays, right?' she said looking out the window and playing with her hair.

"Well, that's a surprise." I said as the radio finally gave me some relief and some old forgotten song started playing serenely.

'Why so?' she asked turning her face towards me as I imagined myself caressing those beautiful black curls.

"Your Boyfriend doesn't take you out or what? *Kanjoos hai ya bikhaari(Is he a miser or a beggar)?'* I asked getting ready for another punch.

'Oh *ha ha ha*, you are so funny Mister. It's not like that, I just don't get the time, that's all.' she retorted.

"Oh really? What was his name again…Sulabh or Simran or Samar?"

'Sahaj….and don't pretend like you forgot, you asshole.' she fumed.

"Kind of a girly name, no? *Sahaj…What's next? Sasural Sahaj ka?*" I said bursting into laughter at my own stupid joke.

'You'll never let this joke get old, will you?' she said slapping me on the head.

"Chill yaar, you give the material, I just deliver!" i said making a peace sign with my fingers.

'Shhh….be quiet. Listen to this song' she said with authority.

'Looks like it's your lucky day, mister.' she said as *Tere mere sapne* from the movie Guide started playing on the radio.

"You remember?" I asked almost surprised that she could recollect my favorite song even after all these years.

'Of course I remember, silly. You never let me forget about it whenever we talk over the phone!' she said egging me with her elbow.

"Yeah, I really love this song." I said quietly after a while, looking at the car steering.

'I know you do, Arjun.' She said keeping her hand on mine. 'I like it too'

For a moment as our eyes met each other, what should have felt like pure joy, gave in to a strange feeling of sadness that swarmed over me.

This is it, buddy. This is all you're ever gonna get out of this arrangement. A pat on the cheek, a soft touch of her hands. Maybe a careless whisper. Maybe nothing more. Maybe nothing, ever.

I shook my hand over the gear as to pretend to be thinking of starting the engine, and she let go of my hand.

"Traffic's a bitch nowadays in Delhi, I mean it's become really bad." I blurted out to change the topic and end my agony.

'Ya, I guess so.' She said quietly looking out the window again.

"So where to, Miss?" I asked as the signal turned green.

'I don't know, wherever you want to go I guess.' She said, still looking outside.

"Umm...okay. How about a movie?"

She turned her gaze towards me and raised an eyebrow as if surprised I didn't have a better idea in mind.

"Okay fine, no movie then. I think I know a place you'll like." I said as I took a sharp right turn.

'The place is about to close, Sir. I cannot let you go in at this time.' said the chowkidar outside the big metal gate, as I continued to make my case.

"Try and understand *bhaiyya,* it's important." I pleaded some more.

'*Kal Subah aayiega aap, subah khula hoga*' *(come tomorrow, it will be open)* he said negating my requests.

After some negotiating and using *Gandhi Ji's* assistance, I convinced him to let us enter and gestured Shreya to come out of the car.

'But only for half an hour *Sir ji*, otherwise I will be in trouble.' the security guard voice trailed behind us as we entered the enclosure.

'You'll never change, you sly creature.' She poked me as we saw the gate close behind us, and I tried to look innocent.

The park was a recently constructed area by the DDA and had become quite the popular spot for everyone around the neighborhood; be it for the oldies for their evening walks or the young ones for their free spirited play. The enclosure was spread over quite a large area, with lush green grass spread everywhere along with beautiful landscaping throughout. The grass was dug up at frequent intervals to make way for exquisite potted flora, the scent of some of which was quite intoxicating, to say the least.

All in all, a nice little shindig for spending a few quiet moments with oneself. We walked around for a while till we found a nice little slant of wet grass and sat down.

'So, this is the best you could think of?' she asked putting her hands on her crossed knees.

"I know you like it, so don't even pretend you don't." I said triumphantly.

'Whatever.' she smiled. 'You don't know everything, you know!' she said trying hard to conceal her defeat.

"I know what I'm supposed to know."

'And that's supposed to mean what, exactly?' she asked putting her closed fist below her chin like a small curious child.

"Nothing, nothing at all." I said casually. "So, you like this place or not?"

'It's nice, not where I had expected I'd be today, so it feels kind of good to be here. The flowers are beautiful.' She said pointing to some nearby blue dandelions that had recently sprouted up.

"Not as beautiful as you though." I said not looking at her and playing with some blades of the wet grass.

'Thanks.' she spoke quietly as she looked at me fleetingly. 'You really think I'm beautiful *ya phir bas aise hi bolta hai? (Or you just say so for the sake of it?)*' she asked, still looking at the grass beneath her feet.

"*Nah*, just passing time." I tilted my head to mock her and she laughed.

"So how's everything going?"

'Everything's okay only, I guess. Semester exams coming soon, so will get busy in a while.'

"How are things with Sahaj?"

'Oh you know, the usual. We went out a few times, it was quite nice. I think I'm growing quite fond of him. He's rather charming, to say the least.' She said with a smile as she flicked the blade of grass she was playing with, into a distance. *That blade of grass is more or less you, buddy...accept it now.*

"So, it seems you're fairly smitten by this chap, then. Lucky guy."

'Oh I think I'm the lucky one here.' She blushed as her wild charms pierced my skin like hot molten snappy needles.

"That's great, I'm happy for you Shreya." I said as she smiled and I held back my gut from violently spewing onto the wet green grass.

We sat there for a while quietly, as gusts of cool wind began to blow across the grass patches. I looked at her, sitting calmly in a white T-shirt and jeans, with her eyes closed as if the heavenly breeze was leaving imprints on her soul. It was a remarkable sight; seeing the girl I had given my heart to, the girl who had also refused to accept it, and the same beautiful girl who was to be someone else's now. Not many things in life hurt as badly as seeing the person who you love more than yourself, wanting to be with somebody other than you, *maybe better than you.* Still, I thought, maybe I'll have *this* memory for the rest of my life. *This* moment would be mine, and nobody else's. *A precious little piece of happiness, just for me.* And maybe it would be one of my last moments with her, considering what I had decided to do now.

'You seem awfully quiet there, doc.' she said coming a little close to me.

"Oh nothing, I'm just…" I wandered off again.

'Just…? Just what, Arjun?'

"Tired." I said meekly without looking at that gorgeous face of hers.

'Are you feeling all right?' she asked, a bit concerned now. 'Let's go home if you want.'

"I'm tired Shreya…tired of not saying what I should have said long ago, and what I should be saying to you every day for the rest of my life. I've grown tired of this inadequate and nagging feeling I get whenever I talk to you over the phone. Being hundreds of miles away from you, dying to hear your voice every day, wanting to see your face just so that I can go to sleep peacefully at night; just knowing that you still are a part of my life, even if you don't belong to me. *That maybe on somedays, you think about me too, in a way that only I can think of you.*" I said looking straight ahead.

'Arjun…I…' she stuttered after pausing for a few seconds.

"I Love You, Shreya Kapoor, *I always have and I always will.* I'm not afraid to say it anymore, and I don't care about the consequences too. At least I won't have to regret this day when you were with me in this moment, and I fell for you all over again, as I have before, every single day of my life." I said finally meeting her regard.

She turned her gaze away from me and clutched her knees with her crossed arms. She sat silently for a while, looking straight ahead and not saying anything.

Went better than I expected. I thought to myself and was quite amazed at my ability to gather black humour surprisingly well, be it at my own expense.

I put my right hand in my pocket and took it out, *the thing that was going to be, quite possibly my last gift for her.* It was a gold plated butterfly shaped pendant I had picked for her a while back. The Butterfly surrounded a purple crystal wedged in between, which had really caught my eye. I opened the chain and put the pendant around her neck from behind.

'Arjun, what's this?' she asked a little alarmed.

"It'll look good only on you and nobody else, so I guess in a way, it was made for you."

'It looks lovely, I guess you chose well for the occasion.' She said trying to smile awkwardly.

"Yeah, I think it's the only thing I'm good at though."

"Shreya, I know you want to be with somebody else and sooner or later, I am going to have to make peace with it. I just wanted you to know this, that I'm not just there in your life, sitting and waiting idly by for you to give me my dues. I have waited for you my whole life, waited so long to tell you the things I just did; be it all for nothing, I don't care. But the one thing I want to tell you the most is, we cannot be friends anymore, Shreya. There is a time limit for everything in life, be it friendship, loyalty or love. Our time limit for being friends has come. *I cannot be a friend to you, anymore.*

A little drizzle had started pouring on our heads during this conversation, and I had a strange feeling of relief as well. *Time to go home, lad. You went big, that you'll always be proud of.*

We sat there for about five minutes or so, neither of us saying anything at all. Shreya was just lost in thought, simply looking at the ground with her fingers feeling encircling the shape of the butterfly around her neck. After sometime, the silence got the better of my patience, and I got up.

"Let's go, it's about to rain." I said looking at the sky, which had turned a dark blue shade now. I thought of offering my hand to help her up, and then regretted the thought.

She kept sitting there in the same pose, as if in shock after having just heard the news of someone close passing away. I shrugged off the blades of grass stuck beneath my brown trousers, and started to walk. After walking a few paces, I turned around to see that she had not moved an inch in the last few minutes.

"You coming?" I called out a bit harshly.

'Yeah, I'm…coming.' she muttered, waking up from her trance.

We made our way across the thick luscious greenery that had look way more pleasant the first time around. As we were reaching the steps leading up to the main exit gate of the park, I felt a gentle grapple on my left hand. It was Shreya, who had grabbed it from behind.

"Something wrong?" I enquired as if the rest of the evening had gone quite right.

'How do you know, that you're in love with me?' she asked still looking down.

"It's Love, not a disease...I cannot give you symptoms, can i?" I retorted thinking about the utter futility of this unnecessary conversation.

'What if, you start feeling this way about someone else? What if, these feelings are just temporary?'

I lifted her face and kept looking into her eyes.

'Can you assure me in some way, that if I were to be yours, nothing would ever come between us?' she asked with what seemed like moist eyes.

"No, I cannot. I cannot give you a warranty period on my feelings. But, i will tell you something. And maybe it's the only thing I am capable of telling you right now. If and when, you do decide to take this leap of faith...I won't ever let you fall. If we are destined to be together in this lifetime, then I promise you, this lifetime will be our Eternity."

She intertwined her fingers with mine and came close to me. She pursed her lips close to my ears and all I could hear or feel for those moments were her blissful sighs.

'There is no Sahaj…*there never was a Sahaj.*' She whispered in my ears after kissing me on the cheek as the expression on my face changed into an amalgamation of shock, anticipation for more shock and cautionary happiness.

"But…I thought…you said that" I started blabbering when she stared into my eyes with a lovely pair of her own.

'You are a *buddhu… and* will always remain a *buddhu*' she said keeping her soft hands on my cheeks and bursting into a teary laughter.

The Security Guard at the exit gate could not comprehend the look I had on my face as we walked out holding hands; and neither could I have possibly understood my own feelings at that time.

When we reached the spot where I had parked my car, I stopped for a while and looked at Shreya. I turned to face her and realized she was blushing as she looked at me. I took both her hands in mine.

"Shreya, ever since I first saw you in that cute ponytail, you have been my life. I have dreamt and dreamt of seeing us together one day. You can't imagine the happiness I feel whenever I see you or talk to you; it's like every fiber of my being yearns for your presence. All I want to say is that, it has dawned upon me without a doubt that I cannot think about, or be with anyone else for the remainder of my life." I said to her as she smiled at me, blushing some more.

"So, before you tell me that you're going to be mine as I'm yours, I really want you to know something." I said as she raised her eyebrows with anticipation.

'Tell me.' She said quietly, moving a tad closer to me.

"Once you're mine, you're mine forever Shreya Kapoor. I'm never letting go. I have lost you once, I won't lose you again." I said, surprising myself with the authority in my voice.

She came close to me and embraced me lovingly. I gently put my arms around her as she pressed her head against my chest.

I heard what felt like silent sobs as she grabbed me tightly. I lifted up her face and gazed into her eyes.

'Forever?' she asked as a small tear drop made its way down to her left cheek. I held her face in both my hands and kissed her on the forehead.

"*Forever.*" I whispered in her ear as the storm clouds above us, burst open with elation.

****

EPILOGUE

'You seem to be doing quite better now, Arjun.' Dr. Solanki said, gazing calmly at me as I sat down in front of her on the soft lush brown sofa in her office.

Dr. Kalpana Solanki was a private psychiatrist I had been seeing for many months now. I had been suffering from major depressive episodes in the initial months after Shreya had passed away, and I had no choice but to start getting counseled by someone with a degree to change my ever suicidal mood. It had seemed futile at first, but the sessions did help somewhat. She had started me on standard Anti-depressants which had done their best to disorient my brain and sleep, but at least after a while I had stopped having the urge to put a fork in my eye. The date was 12th of February 2011, and it had been almost nine months since Shreya had left me.

"Well doc, I do feel good. I don't even mind coming here now and then for my crazy pills." I laughed as she joined me with a chuckle.

'You have been bulking up too, I see. I'm glad you're getting some workout, Arjun. *A healthy mind lives in a healthy body, you know.*' She said as I smiled politely.

'Now, about your medicines. You wanted to ask me some questions regarding them?' she asked as I nodded.

"I did, *doc*. Well, what exactly is going to happen if I stop taking them abruptly?"

'Why do you ask? Have you stopped taking them ,Arjun? You know that won't be good for you.'

"Obviously I haven't stopped, *doc*. I'm just curious. You know, just in case I miss a dose here and there." I asked with clasped hands.

'Missing one or two won't bother you much. Missing a lot of them could turn out very unpleasant for you. You might start having rapid mood swings, episodes of rage, abnormal behavior or get even more depressed than before.'

"Unpleasant, you say?" I asked as she looked at her drug chart.

'Yes Arjun. But I don't think you would want to hamper the progress you've been making in the past few months now, isn't it?'

"Of course, *doc*. I'd never think of doing that." I said with a smile.

I came out of her office and hastily crossed the road to get a smoke from a nearby tea stall. I sat down on one of the wooden benches, and took a deep drag; the familiarity of nicotine waking up my lungs and senses. I was about halfway done with it, when I felt my phone vibrate in my jeans. *It had arrived.* I took the phone out of my pocket and checked the inbox messages folder. The message had read -

Here's what I could find. Details and address enclosed.

Make it even, my old friend.

The cigarette between my fingers had almost burnt out by then, as I took one last drag and flicked it to the ground.

I stood up and got a sudden head rush, a rush that felt good after a long, long time. As I opened my wallet to pay for the pack of lights, I saw Shreya's old photograph still embedded in the front pocket, where it had always been. A rare smile spread across my face as I paid the vendor, and turned around to leave.

"Forever, my love." I whispered into the cold evening breeze, and made my way across the busy street.

****

ABOUT THE AUTHOR

Anant Parasher is a budding young doctor who has just completed MD Medicine at Assam Medical College, Dibrugarh. An avid reader of short fiction and literature, this is his first tryst with storytelling. He resides with his family in Gurgaon, Haryana.

He can be reached via his Facebook Page or via email at *anant02jan@gmail.com*

www.ingramcontent.com/pod-product-compliance
Lightning Source LLC
Chambersburg PA
CBHW032003170626
46807CB00006B/2617